ARCTIC
LEGACY

ARCTIC LEGACY

•

LORETTA JACKSON
&
VICKIE BRITTON

AVALON BOOKS
NEW YORK

PRINTED IN THE UNITED STATES OF AMERICA
ON ACID-FREE PAPER
BY HADDON CRAFTSMEN, BLOOMSBURG, PENNSYLVANIA

To Darlyne Stanley,
who travelled with us in Alaska

With thanks to Antoinette Sitting Up

Chapter One

A tall, slender man with hair streaked golden by the sun walked past the bus. As Ara's eyes met his through the foggy window, the young man smiled and raised a hand in comradely greeting, as if they were meeting on some isolated Alaskan trail instead of in the bustling port of Seward.

Ara watched him as he headed toward the bay, steps quick and free, head held high, unmindful of the fine rain. He soon disappeared from her view, lost among the boats that jammed the docks.

Ara continued to gaze after him. In the space of that very brief encounter, the passing stranger had made a strong impression on her. He looked like a man straight out of Robert Service's poems, the kind Alaska calls to, one of the "strong and the sane." That

1

was the exact way she imagined her father, who Ara would meet this morning for the first time.

Ara left the bus slowly, her way blocked by an elderly lady who had stopped to shuffle through her belongings for hat and umbrella. Once outside, as indifferent to the windswept drizzle as the stranger had been, Ara waited for the bus driver to unload her duffel bag. As she did, she glanced toward a small group of people huddled under the awning of a nearby shop. All of them were tourists, she decided, embarking or disembarking from one of the cruise ships. None of them even remotely resembled the photo of her father she carried in her shoulder-strap bag.

She had all but memorized the letter she had received from him in answer to her first contact. "Enclosed you will find a pass. Just go ahead and board the ship and I will join you there. You'll get a chance to see the real Alaska from the deck of the *Sea Rogue,* and the trip along the beautiful coastline will give us a chance to get acquainted."

She walked quickly, attention focused on the names of the vessels, keeping watch for one lettered the *Sea Rogue.* She had mused a long time over that name. She couldn't help thinking it might well describe the man she was to meet.

Ara finally spotted it. Larger, bulkier than she had expected, it towered above the surrounding craft. Compared to the fancy tour-line cruiser anchored beside it, the *Sea Rogue* looked like some battered old tramp. The black paint on the thick, iron sides was weathered, pitted by salt and streaked by rust. But the huge red name, the *Sea Rogue,* glared out proudly, as if to announce to the world that it had battled many a storm and that it would be doing so long after the fancy ships around it had been permanently docked.

The drops of rain became larger and began falling faster. Ara ducked under the cover of a boathouse and hoisted her duffel bag up beside her on the bench beneath it. She glanced at her watch. She would just wait here for a while and see if she would recognize her father, who would surely be looking for her.

Time passed. She drew the photograph from her purse, the one her mother had pressed into her hand shortly before she had died.

''I wanted you to know from the first. But Melvin kept saying you would be better off if you thought we were your real parents. He insisted it would be to your advantage to believe a lie, but I know now that we should have told you. You were not born to us. We adopted you when you were a baby.''

Ara had been far too shocked to make any reply. Her lovely socialite mother, her banker father, her well-ordered life in the small town of Silver Lake, Montana, seemed to fly all out of focus.

''My little sister, Rhonda, fell in love with a man the family didn't approve of,'' her mother, Betty had told her. ''They ran off and got married. Since Rhonda was underage, Dad brought her back, had the marriage annulled, and got a restraining order against your father. Dad really hated him.''

''Why?''

She had shrugged. ''Your father, Sam Neely, was

one of those wanderers. He rejected all the values we live by. I suppose that was why Father detested him so much, but there could have been more to it than that.''

''What about . . . Rhonda? What was she like?''

''Even though she died shortly after you were born, I always tried to keep her memory alive for you. She was everything I've always told you she was, pretty, smart, daring. If she hadn't been so daring, she wouldn't have been on that speedboat and wouldn't have died so tragically.''

''Did Sam Neely know about me?''

''As far as I know Rhonda never had a chance to tell him. We kept the story a well-guarded secret. My husband and I decided to adopt you, and we've loved you as our very own child.''

Tears filled Ara's eyes. After graduating from college, Ara had stayed in Silver Lake during her mother's final illness. She realized she would never be able to travel far enough away to evade the terrible grief she felt.

Rain pelted the wooden roof above her. Water streamed through cracks and settled in puddles on the uneven cement at her feet.

''Ara, you're the last of our family. That means you are all alone; you have no one now. That's why I want you to know the truth. Whether you look him up or not is up to you, but the man in this picture is your father.''

Ara stared down at the crumpled photograph. Sam Neely couldn't be her father. Her father had been a bank president back in Silver Lake, Montana. She didn't feel any connection between herself and the man who smiled, white teeth flashing, in the picture. Except, perhaps, for the fact that he looked like an adventurer, and a desire for adventure had always flared inside Ara, had caused her to choose the outdoor life as her career. She wanted to see and experience the world for herself. This wanderer spirit must be in her blood, must have, more than anything else, brought her to this faraway port in Alaska.

But Ara certainly didn't look like Sam Neely. Her long black hair was straight; his hair and beard tended to curl. His stocky build suggested strength and endurance; Ara's slender one matched her clear-cut, chiseled features. His broad face had weathered early—in the photo he couldn't have been much more than twenty. But what did he look like now? Would she even be able to recognize him?

"Lady."

Startled, Ara looked around. She had not heard anyone approach.

"Lady. Do you have a little cash to spare?"

The man she faced was dressed in a ragged black jacket that was soaking wet. His emaciated frame, shivering a little, remained immobile. It was hard to determine his age. His thin face was covered by whiskers. The deep creases there, like gashes from scars, might have been caused from constant squinting into glaring sea or brilliant snow.

He held out a hand as if he had some rightful claim on the contents of her purse.

For an instant Ara felt half-afraid of him. No doubt he only wanted money for booze. She started to reject his request, but thought of her father roaming alone in Alaska, facing who knew what, and drew out a few bills.

The salty-looking old man didn't even say thank-you. In fact, he didn't say anything else, just trudged off, probably to some tavern sunk among the stores that lined the harbor.

Ara heard a short, appreciative laugh from behind her.

The same blond-haired man who had passed by the bus stood just beyond the protection of the roof. He was regarding her, blue eyes glinting with humor. When she didn't speak, he joked, ''Do you have a couple of bucks left for me?''

Ara, again aware of the sense of comradeship she had felt upon first seeing him, smiled.

He stepped out of the rain under the boathouse's extended roof. His white T-shirt was damp and clung to his broad chest. His thick blond hair glistened with moisture.

''Out here you never know when fortunes will change. You may be the one down on your luck some-day, and that very man may come by and pay you back threefold.''

''I don't think I'll wait for that to happen.''

He laughed, a short, quick laugh that made him look appealing and carefree.

Ara glanced in the direction the beggar had taken. ''Have you ever seen him before?''

"I've seen the likes of him before. Here in Alaska lots of guys wander around aimlessly in search of . . ." His voice trailed off. "In search of . . . it's hard to say what . . . but it isn't just a free meal."

"Have you been in Alaska long?" Ara asked him.

"I was born in Anchorage. Twenty-six years ago. Where do you come from?"

"Montana."

"Just a little rich girl, out seeing the sights, I guess."

Rich, yes, Ara was. She was sole heir to the Londell money. But that didn't mean that she wanted to live a life of leisure. Ara loved the field she had chosen; she felt alive working with wildlife, with all that concerned the environment. She intended to become deeply involved in her field. "Not sight-seeing," Ara replied. "I've been offered a job as a biological technician at Lake Clark National Park. That is, if I decide to remain here. I told them I would give them my decision in a week or two."

"They say Alaska's a place you either love or hate at first sight. Few come to stay. Most of them can't get out of here fast enough."

"It's a beautiful place. I just might be one of those who stay."

"I must warn you," he said, slanting her a skeptical gaze, "Alaska isn't for sissies."

"What makes you think I am one?" she demanded with a proud lift of her chin.

He laughed in the same lighthearted way. "I'll

check with you again this winter, when it gets twenty below.''

Ara could have countered that it got plenty cold in Montana, too. But she said nothing. Their eyes locked and Ara felt a little breathless. She found it difficult to look away.

''But to do that,'' he said, ''I'll need to know your name.''

''Ara Londell.''

''I'm Marc Stewart. From Seward. That's almost a poem, isn't it?''

''Not a very good one.''

He took a step backward, once again buffeted by large drops of rain. ''Maybe our paths will cross again,'' he said before he turned and walked off.

Watching his departure, Ara felt a sharp sense of disappointment. Back at the university and at home in Silver Lake she had met many would-be suitors. None of them had interested her for long. Most of them seemed so narrow, their lives already deeply rutted in routine. But Marc appeared so different from any of them. She wished they had exchanged phone numbers or planned some way to contact each other again.

Ara glanced with impatience down the long walkway toward the *Sea Rogue*. No one who could possibly be her father stood watching from the deck. A slender man with lank, reddish hair seemed to be in charge. He stood by idly, giving directions to crew hands transporting cargo.

It struck her as odd that her father would suggest that they meet for the first time on some freighter. Of course, she didn't mind—it looked more adventurous than the fancy tour liners—but it was indeed strange that he hadn't arrived by now and that he wasn't actively seeking her.

Unless Sam Neely had already boarded and was waiting for her inside one of the cabins.

Ara waited a while longer, watching the gulls, watching the well-dressed passengers who boarded the nearby cruiser. As she did, the entire venture began to appear to be a sad mistake. She wondered why she had ever contacted him. No doubt her grandfather had been entirely justified in his hatred. Worthless as a youth, her father had probably after all these years become totally shiftless, like that man begging for a handout. Who knew? Maybe the beggar she had just given money to was her father. Maybe he had just wanted to see her, and that was all.

Ara checked her watch—five minutes until eleven. She must either board or catch a bus back to her hotel in Anchorage. With grave reservations she lifted her duffel and headed toward the *Sea Rogue*.

The rain had let up some, but still made little rivulets as it hit against the sea.

The red-haired man she had noticed from a distance, who seemed to be in charge, was now leaning, elbows on the railing, gazing down into the water. He was probably in his late thirties. As she drew closer, she saw that he had a foreign look about him. She guessed that he was either Norwegian or Dutch.

Ara walked up the loading plank and started past him.

She wasn't aware that the sailor had even noticed her until he spoke. His words, heavily accented, had a sharp, even rude, ring. "Where are you going?"

Ara turned back, opened her purse, and showed him her pass.

His fair skin was freckled, and his pale green eyes, overly bold, almost insolent, made Ara uncomfortable.

"We don't take many passengers. Who gave this to you?"

"Sam Neely."

He looked surprised, then quickly handed the paper back to her and turned away. He no longer seemed to be the same man who had been lingering lazily on deck for the last half hour. Now he appeared on edge, pressed for time.

"Wait," Ara said. "Have you seen Mr. Neely? Is he on board?"

"No," the sailor answered shortly. "And he's not likely to be. We're launching in a few minutes." He did not glance back at her, but entered a door marked LOWER LEVEL: NO ADMITTANCE.

Not on board—that was to be the state of her relationship with her newly found father.

Moisture hung heavily over the old craft, maximized the smell of salt, of fish, of diesel oil. Assailed by these scents, Ara felt a little queasy.

She moved over to the edge of the ship, standing in the same spot where the sailor had stood only a few minutes ago. She, like him, gazed down into the water of the bay. There she remained. Deckhands released the thick ropes that bound the old freighter to the dock;

the heavy metal side door creaked as it raised and closed. She had lost her chance to get off.

Ara watched as the *Sea Rogue* chugged slowly away from port, sending sprays of water in its wake.

The crew had moved on to other duties, leaving Ara alone, solitary. She wondered if she were the only passenger on board. Ara thought of Silver Lake, Montana, and of the hospital where she had kept her weary vigil. The pain of her great loss returned stronger than ever, and added to it was an even greater loneliness.

Nothing could change one clear fact: Sam Neely had abandoned her just the way he had abandoned her mother twenty-two years ago.

Chapter Two

As the *Sea Rogue* chugged away from the port, Ara continued to gaze down the ship's rusty side into the water. She remained, watching Seward disappear and mountains rise on either side of the bay.

She should have stayed in Anchorage and refused to take this voyage to . . . to where? It didn't really seem to matter. The plans she had made back in Montana, made with such excitement and expectation, had already been dashed to bits.

Feeling great frustration, she swung around. At the same moment the foreign sailor returned to the deck from the door marked NO ADMITTANCE. Behind him followed a man in his sixties, suave and dignified, with trim gray hair and mustache.

Both of them drew to a stop when they saw her. She could not understand the foreign sailor's hostility.

12

He spoke in an undertone to his companion, words she could not hear. The older man's dark eyes raised to her as he listened.

The sailor ducked into the center area enclosed by thick, murky glass. The other man approached her in an unwelcoming way as if it ran contrary to his plans to have her aboard.

Nevertheless, first and foremost a gentleman, he extended his hand, saying, "I'm Farley Riggs, captain of the *Sea Rogue.*"

He looked far too sophisticated to be in charge of such an impoverished old boat. "Ara Londell," she replied, and showed him her pass.

Farley Riggs inspected the paper in a way that suggested it was his custom to give great consideration to everything he saw and heard. "We don't often take passengers. We've admitted only one family today, who will disembark at Lone Port." He eyed her, dark eyes serious and thoughtful. "Where are you going?"

His question caused her to hesitate, to feel a little foolish. "I'm not familiar with your schedule."

"This craft is what is called a tramp. Which means we do not run regularly between fixed ports. Our final destination this trip is Kotzebue, in the Arctic Circle."

"Actually, I'm looking for Sam Neely."

The captain gave another long, calculated pause. "You won't find him here."

"Where would I find him?"

"An often-asked question." After a few minutes of silence, he went on. "I've worked for Sam Neely for the past sixteen years. But not on this old tub. My usual run is a cruise ship called the *Midnight Sun.*''

''You work for . . . him?'' In the silence that followed Ara attempted to rearrange all of her preconceived notions. She had pictured Sam Neely as irresponsible, as penniless and destitute. She had even gone so far as to wonder if her father had been the vagabond who had asked her for money.

''The regular captain of the *Sea Rogue* quit without notice just a few weeks ago. That really put Sam in a bind. So I'm filling in until he can find a suitable replacement.''

Still unable to believe they were speaking of the same person, she qualified, ''You mean Sam Neely *owns* this ship?''

The natural arch of dark eyebrows raised at her question. ''Mr. Neely owns an entire fleet of ships. He heads Wayfarer Charters, one of the finest charter companies in Alaska.''

Ara's spirits lifted over hearing the news. Sam Neely had struck it rich in Alaska, had become owner of a thriving business. That must surely mean that because of business interferences, he had been delayed. He would meet her somewhere down the line. ''What is our next stop?''

''We travel straight through the night to Lone Port. There we drop anchor for a spell.'' As if distracted by the thought of some unattended responsibility, he started away, stopping to say as he gestured toward the glass-paneled enclosure, ''The cabins are through the dining hall to the left.'' He handed her a key. ''You may have the third one, in the center.''

After stowing her luggage in the tiny, dismal room, Ara wandered back to the dining area.

The surly red-haired sailor lounged on a bench near the entrance to the dining room.

''What would cause you to board an old freighter like this one?'' he demanded in his choppy accent. ''Just where are you going?''

She did not like his rude manner. She did not like him, the offensive glint of pale green eyes, his thick lips, slack and moist. ''I'm heading for . . .'' Ara had to stop and try to recall the boat's destination. ''For Kotzebue.''

''Not much there,'' he said, his tone almost mocking, as if he had recognized her answer to be one she had just invented.

''What is your job?'' she asked, forcing herself to be friendly.

''I'm Hal Bruins. I am the cook and the captain bold.'' He laughed at his own cleverness.

''Not the captain,'' she corrected pleasantly. ''I've just met him.''

Hal shot back, his tone serious, ''I am first mate, chief steward, and purser.''

For having all those titles, if indeed he did, Hal Bruins certainly appeared to have a lot of idle time on his hands.

''With all those jobs, I must do a lot of thinking,'' he said, tapping the side of his head.

''I had better let you get back to your work then,''

Ara replied, walking on. She could feel his penetrating gaze still on her and again felt disturbed by his open antagonism.

Ara stopped and poured coffee into one of the Styrofoam cups, then turned to gaze around the room. The dark gray paint and the cloudy windows made it immensely dreary. She looked at the thick, heavy tables and benches, all bolted to the floor, and thought that the old craft must not be given to smooth sailing.

The passengers the captain had spoken of sat quietly at a far table, a huge Indian man and his pretty wife. Two small children sat on the floor at their feet spinning empty pop cans.

Ara's gaze wandered on and was met by a friendly smile. The girl, who must be around her own age, had a beaming, shiny face and windblown blond hair. She was seated across from a young man, who seemed far too well dressed for the *Sea Rogue.*

"Join us," the girl called out with enthusiasm.

"I'm Ara Londell," she said as she seated herself beside the man, who had slid over to make room for her.

"I'm Pat," the affable blond girl replied, "and this, this handsome man, is my"—her voice rose with the pretense of putting on airs—"is my *fiancé,* Curtis Carter."

Ara couldn't help thinking how mismatched the two of them looked. Pat, wearing a denim blouse and baggy shorts, definitely belonged to Alaska, at home on this boat. Her fiancé did not. Despite the sunglasses pushed back into the crest of brown hair, he looked far too immaculate, as if he had been transplanted here out of some vital New York office.

But he was very attractive in a wholesome, clean-shaven way—small nose, very earnest hazel eyes. His longish hair didn't go along with the rest of his appearance; Ara wondered if he had let it grow to please Pat.

"What brings you aboard the *Sea Rogue*?" Pat asked.

Ara tried to answer just as casually. "I am looking for Sam Neely."

Pat's exuberance seemed to drain away at the mention of his name. The couple exchanged glances. Some unspoken communication passed between them that caused Ara to feel an increased anxiety.

"I expected him to be on this voyage," Ara went on, wary now, measuring the reaction of her words.

Pat's eyes did not sparkle as they had before. "Why are you looking for him?"

Before Ara could answer, Curt spoke up. "I work for Sam Neely, as general manager of Wayfarer Charters. If it's a business manner, maybe I can be of help."

Ara shook her head. "No, I will need to see him. This is . . . personal."

"Then talk to me," Pat spoke up. "I'm a Neely. I'm Sam's niece."

The announcement took Ara totally by surprise. She had thought only of meeting her father; she had not considered the possibility that Sam had family here in Alaska.

Ara observed Pat, looking for signs of Neely blood. Pat's blondness, her fair skin, sprinkled lightly with freckles, served to mask any resemblance to Sam Neely. But on closer look, the girl's robust frame, her features, slightly irregular, did in some way put her in mind of her father's photograph.

Ara considered telling Pat, her newly found half cousin, exactly who she was, but quickly thought better of it. Sam Neely had obviously not told Pat anything about her. If Ara had been amazed to hear Sam had a niece, imagine how shocked Pat would be to find out he had a long-lost daughter!

It would take time for Pat to believe the story and to accept her. In the meantime it would be best not reveal her identity, not until she had spoken with her father.

"How would I go about contacting him?"

"Our main office is in Seward, but we also have offices in Nome and Kotzebue." As Curt spoke, he shot another guarded glance toward Pat.

Pat seemed to defy him this time. "My uncle hasn't been seen at any of his offices for over a week," she blurted out.

"Now, don't go getting upset. His leaving for a spell without telling anyone isn't really that unusual for him, now, is it, Pat?"

"Sam usually calls me. But this time he just took off without a word to anyone."

They sat in silence for a while, Curt toying with the can of Coke, Ara taking a drink of coffee. The coffee, strong and bitter, was difficult to swallow.

Pat, unmindful of her drink and the chips that lay beside it, gazed grimly toward the doorway. Suddenly she called out, "Marc! Am I glad to see him! Maybe he knows something!"

Ara glanced around. Marc Stewart, the attractive stranger she had talked to while onshore, had entered the dining room. Ara had not expected to see him again, least of all aboard the *Sea Rogue*. For a moment his intense blue eyes met hers, and she felt a little breathless just as she had back in Seward.

"Hello, Ara!" he said with a warm smile. "Our paths cross again."

Curtis addressed him, not too happily. "I didn't expect to see you on board."

"This is my vacation," Marc replied, seating himself across from Ara, beside Pat. "I thought I'd go up to Nome, see to a little business up there, and then go on to Kotzebue. Might be nice for a change to leave all the responsibility to Captain Riggs."

"Are you a sea captain?" Ara asked.

"No, a pilot. A bush pilot, if you will."

Pat gripped his arm. "Marc, I'm worried about Sam."

Marc's brows knitted, giving a craggy look to his face. "I am too, Pat. I guess that's the real reason I'm taking this trip."

Pat's fingers tightened around his wrist. "Do you think he's wrecked somewhere? Do you think he's been in an accident?"

"I just don't know, Pat. I called the Coast Guard just this morning. He was last seen leaving Nome early

Friday morning in that small craft of his, *Arctic Night.* They've searched high and low, but neither he nor the boat has been found.''

A vision arose to Ara, the small vessel sunk, her father drowned in the icy waters of Nome. The lingering picture of an empty sea, of a total void, terrified her. She felt her heart constrict as she quickly left the table.

Ara did not remember the details of getting back out on deck, only that she was again standing at the railing, gazing in horror down at the sea. Her father— missing, maybe even dead. Tears stung her eyes.

''Ara.''

She turned to Marc, who had followed her. She couldn't help stepping toward him, being enfolded in his arms.

''What is it, Ara?'' She leaned against his shoulder, unable to keep from sobbing. All the while Marc's hand smoothed her hair in a gesture of comfort.

''What's wrong? Why are you crying?''

''Sam Neely,'' she said, her words muffled by his jacket. ''He's my father.''

She shouldn't have told him or anyone, but she had. Marc listened quietly as she explained to him about their plans to meet each other on this ship.

''Ara, Sam's an experienced sailor. Just because he's missing doesn't necessarily mean he's met with disaster.''

''How do you explain the fact that he's been missing for so long? That no one can find him?''

Marc's words consoled her. ''Sam's done this kind

of thing before. He's not one for calling home or for punching clocks."

"You must know him very well."

"We're both in the charter business. I do my work in the air; he in the sea. We're good friends." His warm hand touched her face as if he wished he could transfer the pain she felt to himself. "Ara, I do intend to find him. So please, please, don't worry."

When Ara returned to the dining room, Pat was gone. So was the unpleasant sailor, Hal Bruins. But she found Curtis still holding his unfinished drink. "I don't know what to do with Pat," he said worriedly as she approached.

Ara sank into the bench across from him just as the captain's deep voice sounded over the intercom. "We are now passing Piedmont Glacier, just off to the left. Its receding from the mountain has created a dry out-wash plain that you can soon view."

"The old man misses his tour groups," Curtis said with a smile.

The two of them watched from the window as the broad glacier came into view and disappeared. Mountain peaks, and a great valley of ice—in June.

"I can't convince Pat that her uncle is acting par for the course. It's just like Sam to take off without a word to anyone."

Curtis fell silent, turning the can around and around in his hand. "Even if he's gotten stranded somewhere, Sam knows how to take care of himself. He's likely to show up anyplace, anytime. Why, I wouldn't be surprised if he turns up in Lone Port.''

Marc and now Curtis's words served to restore her. Ara continued to gaze from the window, Pat's absence placing an awkwardness between them.

''You've known Sam Neely for some time. Can you tell me anything about him?''

Curtis studied Ara, his hazel eyes growing dark. ''I'm in charge of managing a good part of the Wayfarer company. And I can tell you this: Sam's in a lot of trouble.''

''Trouble?'' Ara repeated with amazement.

''I don't suppose I should be talking about it, but Wayfarer Charters is in real jeopardy.'' As he spoke, Curtis kept glancing toward the door leading to the deck. Ara could see he was watching Pat, who was standing outside talking to Marc. As if hurrying so he could confide all before Pat came back in, he pressed on. ''Creditors calling, lawyers, even an IRS agent snooping around.''

''The company must be in financial trouble.''

''Yes, and lots of it. Pat's not much for business, and refuses even to listen to me when I try to tell her. 'Oh, he'll come out of it,' she says, 'he always does.' But this time I'm not so sure.''

This new information again threw Ara off balance. She didn't quite know what to say. Curtis went on without her prompting. ''In fact, the reason I caught a ride on the *Sea Rogue* was to straighten out some business over in Seward, to talk about getting an extension on a loan. I brought Pat with me because she's worried sick about her uncle and refuses to listen to the truth.'' Curtis looked even gloomier. ''Sam's timed this fiasco just in time to ruin our marriage plans.''

''When are you getting married?''

''We had set the date. It was to be right away, the minute we got back to Kotzebue. Now everything's on hold until she finds out her uncle is OK.'' Curtis again lapsed into a moody silence. ''I guess whatever Pat decides, I'll go along with. I just want her to be happy.''

Ara couldn't help admiring Curtis's devotion to Pat and the appealing protectiveness she had noticed from the beginning. He reminded her of the boys Mother had always pressured her to date back home.

''But you do expect Sam Neely to show up? Soon?''

''Maybe I'm just hoping he will. Sam's really left me holding the bag.'' Curtis cast another worried glance in Pat's direction, then shook his head. ''With all that's going on with the company, it's no wonder Sam Neely jumped ship, so to speak.''

Chapter Three

Ara stood on deck breathing deeply of the salty air, refreshed by the sights and smells of the ocean. The ship passed close to protruding cliffs, and Ara spotted a bald eagle nesting high on a rocky promenade. Far, far below him an old sea lion lay sunning himself. What magnificent scenes, perfect shots to add to her collection. She hurried to her cabin for her camera.

Ara returned quickly, the new 35 millimeter she had purchased before leaving Montana hanging from a strap around her neck. Just in time. Ahead of her puffins swarmed around the shallow inlet between gapping canyon walls. Some were walking with stiff, waddling gaits; others bobbed in the still water of the small bay and dived for fish. With a skillful motion she adjusted the lens and zeroed in on a solitary puffin who had ventured out farther than the others. With his

24

large, triangular beak, he looked like a black-and-white parrot.

After she'd taken several more photos of these quaint birds, her attention was caught by the flap of wings overhead. Not a gull, but some kind of bird she had never seen before. She raised her camera and whirled to catch the gliding figure, when she noticed someone standing behind her on the ship's bow.

Ara's sudden turning caused him to draw back. Before he jerked his head away from her, their eyes met for a bare instant, his growing large and startled. Then, faster than the flight of the bird she had been watching, the man slipped through the door that led to the ship's lower level.

His broad, bearlike form seemed familiar; so did the thick, black hair that curled beneath the sailor's cap.

Momentarily frozen to the spot, Ara stared toward the closed door. Either it was her imagination or the man she had just glimpsed bore a striking resemblance to the photo she carried in her purse.

Sam Neely might have been on board from the first, remaining out of sight during these long hours at sea. But why would her father suggest that they meet on the *Sea Rogue*, then do his best to hide from her?

Ara had to find out. Ignoring the warning sign, NO ADMITTANCE, she opened the door and gazed down the stairs leading to the ship's cargo hold. During her cautious descent, she could hear more distinctly the old ship's powerful engine and feel the force of steel cutting through water.

The huge, open compartment in the innermost belly

of the ship was dark, the air layered with heat and oil. She could make out the vague shapes of crates and boxes of varying sizes stacked along the walls.

Ara took another step forward, then drew to a halt, scanning the cluttered area for some sign of motion to break the lifeless solitude. The furtive man who had resembled her father's picture couldn't simply have vanished.

Spotting another door, Ara made her way around crates toward it. She tried to raise the metal latch, but it held firmly in place.

The heavy clack of footsteps sounded behind her. Whoever was with her in the room was making no effort to conceal his presence. She recognized the choppy accent and knew who she would see before she was able to whirl around.

"Just what are you doing down here?"

Hal Bruins's pale eyes bulged with anger. Looming above her in the semidarkness, he looked larger, stockier than he had before. He took a menacing step closer.

Ara struggled for something to say. She couldn't tell him she had been following a man who looked like her father. Instead she managed, "I must have taken a wrong turn somewhere."

Ara started to walk around him, but Hal Bruins moved to the side to block her way.

Ara's heart sank. They were down in this dark hold all alone. No one had seen her enter. Her gaze slipped to the door through which she had entered, and she wondered if he had locked it behind him. If so, she was trapped!

Tensely she waited, intent on showing no fear of him. Hal remained where he was without motion, glaring at her in an undeniably hostile fashion.

His gaze slowly dropped to the camera around her neck. ''There is nothing to take pictures of down here.''

Then he did move, quickly, grabbing at her. Ara tried to evade him, but strong hands locked around her arm. He half-dragged her to the entrance, pushing her ahead of him up the steps.

Once he had opened the door to the deck, he adamantly pointed out the sign. ''Can't you read good, plain English? That says 'No Admittance.' That means you!''

Evicted from the lower level, Ara stared toward the door Hal Bruins had slammed shut between them. His impudent words, still ringing in her ears, added fuel to her anger.

He wasn't going to keep her from finding out whether or not the man she had glimpsed had been her father. She could do nothing about finding him now, but she would continue her search at the first opportunity.

''Ara, I've been looking for you.'' Marc Stewart, handsome in a white sweatshirt and jeans, was striding toward her. Despite her anger and frustration, she was able to face him with a small smile.

He stopped short and, seeing her camera, said, ''How did I know you would be a photographer?''

"I love wildlife. At home I have albums filled with birds and animals."

He gave her an approving look, one that acknowledged that he, too, cared about the things she loved. "You'll have a complete collection before you leave Alaska."

She followed him as he walked over to the railing. They stood side by side, listening to the cry of the gulls that circled overhead.

Ara, still feeling deeply shaken, gave in to her desire to trust him. "I think I saw my father a while ago."

Marc regarded her with surprise and disbelief. "Ara, that's impossible!"

He sounded so adamant that she felt doubt beginning to form in her mind. "The man I saw looked a lot like the picture he gave me, a large man with black hair."

"Sam's hair is turning a little gray," Marc said, as if this fact alone would convince her. Then all of a sudden his frown faded. "I know who you saw. Buddy Walker, one of the deckhands. He's half-Indian, as big as an Alaskan grizzly." Marc's enthusiasm for the idea grew. "Did he try to avoid you?"

"Yes."

"That's because he's . . ." Marc paused. "He's . . . different. Not crazy, mind you. Buddy just doesn't get along well in social situations."

Ara looked away from him, out across the sea, brilliant with sunshine. Maybe she had just wanted to see her father so much that she had grasped at straws. In spite of being nearly convinced by Marc's explanation, she found herself asking, "What do you know about Hal Bruins?"

Again Marc looked surprised. "Not much, really. Hal hasn't worked for Sam all that long. But he came highly recommended—an asset to any skipper who wants to run a tight ship."

"I don't trust him," Ara said.

Once again Ara noted the incredulous look he slanted her. "Do you know what I think? I think you need to get off this ship for a while. Actually, that's why I was looking for you. We'll be docking at Lone Port soon. Would you go with me into town? We'll order some steaks at Maureen's Café and I'll show you a typical Athabascan village."

"I'd love to."

Marc started away, then called back happily over his shoulder, "Don't dress for dinner."

The tiny settlement of Lone Port sank deep into a valley cut between high peaks. It consisted mostly of a scattering of white frame buildings, but in the far distance Ara could see the cupola of an ancient Russian Orthodox church.

The air was crisp and sharp as they strolled along. "Lone Port used to be just an Athabascan fishing camp. But then they put in the salmon cannery and more people started moving in."

He stopped walking. "The cannery's right over there."

At the point where the river joined the sea stood a giant, shedlike structure that looked badly deteriorated from the elements. Even though they were a block or so away, Ara could smell the sharply strong odor of fish.

"I have an Indian friend, Mike, who works there. He says he wears cuffs with chains, so his hands won't get in the way of the sharp blades that cut off the fish heads. During the winter Mike's the cannery's only employee. They keep him on as security guard."

"I don't know whether that makes him lucky or not. This must be a forsaken place when the snows start."

Marc answered with a smile. "They do get weathered in."

Ahead of them, the first people they had spotted, several Indian youths, had gathered near an old building.

"Community store," Marc told her.

"The center of activity," Ara observed.

Marc spoke to the youths in a friendly way. They returned his greeting shyly.

"Just ahead is Maureen's. Believe me, she serves the best apple pie from Washington to the North Pole."

Ara's spirits had begun to lift. Leaving the *Sea Rogue* had given her an entirely different outlook. Confinement on that dreary old freighter was causing her to imagine wild plots and hidden secrets. Even the thought of Hal's evicting her had started to take on a tinge of humor.

"Don't any roads lead out of here?"

"Not far out. The Bering Sea and the river, a tributary of the Yukon, provide major transportation in and out. And of course, small planes, floaters, and skis.'' As he spoke, Marc opened the door to a plain, unadorned restaurant with a handmade sign in the window reading MAUREEN'S CAFÉ.

A wood-burning stove sent a pleasant warmth around the room. People sat in small groups talking and eating. An older man huddled near the counter drinking coffee in a slow, thoughtful manner.

All of them knew Marc. After he had greeted them, and they had taken a side booth, Ara gazed around at the decorations on the walls. On one side of the room hung a moose head; on the other, a shaggy, fierce Alaskan grizzly.

''Maureen's husband was a hunter,'' Marc told her. ''He died eight or ten years ago, but Maureen's stayed on here. Travelers like me find her place a haven.''

''Living out here alone must be tough going.''

Marc laughed. ''You haven't met *tough* until you meet Maureen.''

The café owner dropped what she was doing to scurry toward them. She was a thin, hard-looking woman, with a face lined by many harsh winters. ''Hello, stranger!'' Quick, dark eyes darted to Ara. ''How did you get anyone so pretty to hang out with the likes of you?''

Maureen didn't offer them a menu, just said gruffly, ''What will it be?''

''Two of your perfect rib-eye steaks and two large slices of the best apple pie I've ever eaten.''

''Flatterer.'' Another glance at Ara. ''Beware of flatterers, that's what I always say. What's your name, anyway? Marc's been out in the woods so long we can't expect him to have any manners.''

"I was getting to the introductions. Maureen Sloan, I'd like you to meet Ara Londell.''

"OK, now that that's behind us, what are you going to have to drink?''

"Coffee for me,'' Marc said, and looked at Ara.

"Do you have tea?''

Maureen was gone only a minute before returning with two steaming mugs.

"There's only one bad thing about tea,'' Marc noted with a smile as Maureen placed Ara's cup in front of her. "It ain't coffee.''

Maureen tossed back, "I'd say, instead, 'It ain't whiskey.' ''

Ara was beginning to unwind, to feel relaxed. She liked the outspoken Maureen and her homey little café. It was a place—indeed a haven—one with time, time to be neighborly, to be friendly, to talk and laugh.

"Marc, introduce Ara to Noatak. She'll enjoy looking at his ivory carvings. His new ones are the best ever.''

Ara glanced toward the slender man seated alone at the counter. He had a thin, hollowed face and dark, glowing Oriental eyes.

"He's Lone Port's local artist,'' Marc explained. "An Inupiat Eskimo from the icy north. I don't know what his name is. Everyone just calls him Noatak, which is the place he hails from.''

"Isn't that far up in the Arctic Circle? How did he get way down here?''

Marc smiled. "How did you get way *up* here?"

Ara's eyes rose to the painting just above their table entitled *Caribou Roaming the Tundra.* "Is this his work?"

"Yes. And in that glass case near him are his carvings. Come on, I'll show you."

Noatak gave a pleasant nod as they drew forward.

"I display his work here," Maureen said, moving forward to join them, "until he gets enough together to take to Anchorage."

Inside the case was some of the finest scrimshaw Ara had ever seen. She leaned closer to study a complete walrus tusk intricately carved with a row of Eskimo figures. Beside it were finely decorated ivory snow goggles with slits for eyes, and a large, smiling mask.

Noatak took out one of his smaller carvings, an elongated seal. "*Inua*," he said. "Animal spirit."

"You have wonderful talent," Ara exclaimed, impressed by his deeply stylized motifs that left her feeling an almost reverent awe.

"It's getting harder and harder for me to get ahold of enough ivory," Noatak told her.

"And you're one of the lucky ones, with Eskimo friends who save you tusks from their hunting." Marc turned to Ara. "Only Eskimos can kill the walrus, you know, and then only for their livelihood."

"That's not fair to the other hunters," Maureen cut in.

"You wouldn't say that if you had seen some of the sights I have," Marc replied. "Once I came across forty-five dead walrus. Some profiteers just out and slaughtered them for the tusks, took what they wanted, and walked away.''

The thought distressed Ara, who planned the main focus of her work in Alaska to center on the preserving of endangered species and the safeguarding of wildlife in need of protection: the bald eagle, the sea otter, the polar bear. Even the seal herd had become national property, to be hunted only under strict government supervision.

Once they returned to their table, Marc talked about the wildlife he encountered in his job as bush pilot.

''Do you run an air taxi?''

''Yes, I take people to faraway places. When I'm not doing that, I deliver supplies.'' Marc paused. ''In the winter the bush pilot's work is crucial to remote areas like this one. When the water freezes, there's no way in but by plane. I've flown in food, medical supplies, just about everything that constitutes an emergency.''

''It sounds like a dangerous job.''

''It can be.''

''Don't be modest,'' Maureen said, coming toward them balancing a tray filled with food. ''Last winter Marc risked his life to fly in here. The place was buried in snow and ice. The antibiotics he brought saved a little girl's life.''

''It wasn't so risky. I had a ski plane and, if you recall, I was able to set down without trouble.''

''That's not the way I heard the story,'' Maureen said. ''An hour after he landed, an ice fog set in. Few people could have landed that plane. Yes, Marc's job is high-risk.'' She paused. ''That's why the handsome lug is still single. He lives on the edge, and that excludes his having a wife and family.''

Maureen set down the steaks. ''Marc had a nice girl once, but he refused to take the final step.''

''Maureen imagines I throw women over, but actually it's the other way around.''

''Don't let him kid you. Marc, here, is a dyed-in-the-wool loner.''

Maureen left, pausing to chat with several grizzled-looking men who had just sat down at the table next to them.

Marc's eyes had not left Ara's face. Suddenly he reached across the table and caught her hand. ''Are you a loner, too? Or is there someone waiting back in Montana?''

''No one,'' Ara answered.

No one was waiting for her there, or anywhere.

Marc and Ara left the café in high spirits, warmed by Maureen's hospitality, satisfied by the delicious meal that ended with warm pie that seemed to melt in the mouth. Outside, the temperature had lowered considerably. At any rate, they stepped from cozy café out into brisk, Alaskan evening.

''Not cold, are you?'' Marc asked.

''I'm fine.''

''Let's walk down to the river then.''

They wound their way through tall pines and spruce on a trail that ended beside a wide bank. The gurgle of water mingled with the rustling sounds of small creatures in the high weeds along the shore. A strange, mournful cry pierced the air, then another.

"What was that?" Ara asked.

"Loons."

Ara listened to their haunting cries, and the death of the mother who had raised her, her missing father, made her feel an overpowering sense of loss.

"What's wrong, Ara?"

"Those sounds. They make me sad, that's all."

"You're shivering. You should have told me you were cold." Marc unzipped his jacket and placed it gently around her. The woolly fleece, still warm from his body, comforted her.

His hands lingered on her shoulders. Then, as if he had thought of a better way to keep her warm, his arms enfolded her.

Ara's thoughts and worries vanished as Marc's lips met hers. For a moment there was only the gentle pressure of his mouth against her own. In the shelter of his strong arms she felt safe, secure, no longer so alone.

The kiss deepened. Almost against her will, Ara felt herself responding. Her own intense reaction startled her. How could such a simple kiss, so thoughtful, so tender, evoke such deep feelings? The last thing she had expected was to be caught up in such a dizzying rush of emotion.

Marc drew her away from him, hands still gripping her shoulders. He gazed deeply into her eyes. "Are you still sad?"

He continued to stare at her, as if he, too, had been thrown off course by the magic.

"Wait here a moment," Marc told Ara as they returned to the harbor.

Still feeling the pressure of his lips on hers, she watched Marc stride away to speak to someone on board a small ship.

Docked beside the *Sea Rogue,* this vessel looked sleek and modern, as if a product of a different age. The man Marc was talking to curiously glanced her way. The two of them seemed deep in some important discussion.

Marc soon returned. "It's all set."

"What's set?"

"Your return passage back to Seward aboard the *North Star.* It leaves Lone Port in half an hour. That will give us plenty of time to get your luggage and get you settled in."

Ara, stunned, did not reply at once. Then she told him firmly, "I'm not going back."

"What do you mean?" Marc demanded. He looked genuinely surprised. "I thought we had agreed. It's best for you to return to Anchorage while I try to locate Sam Neely."

Ara, for the first time, found herself bombarded by suspicions of him. She had assumed they had met in Seward by accident. What if everything had been very carefully planned? Marc's offer to help her might be only a hoax, his real goal being to *prevent* her from locating her father.

"I came up here to find my father," she told him, "and I'm not going back until he's found."

A muscle tightened in Marc's jaw. "I'm afraid I must insist."

Ara, not giving him time to go on trying to convince her, started walking toward the *Sea Rogue*.

She could hear Marc calling after her, "Ara, wait!"

Reluctantly, doubting him more than ever, she turned toward him again.

"Don't get back on board, Ara," Marc said. "If you do, you'll be making a big mistake."

Chapter Four

Ara had second thoughts the moment she reboarded the *Sea Rogue*. She remained on the deck facing Lone Port and wondered if she should have listened to Marc and headed back to Anchorage. He had been so insistent, so deadly insistent, almost as if he believed that her journey northward toward the Arctic Circle was going to result in disaster.

But what would cause him to think that? Did Marc know something about Sam Neely he wasn't telling her, something that made him believe searching for him would place Ara in danger?

Her thoughts concerning Marc were not the only source of her uneasiness. Ara glanced back over her shoulder. Her eyes skimmed the area of the deck, skimmed the empty portholes and windows. She couldn't get over the feeling that from somewhere hostile eyes were watching her.

After a little while the feeling began to fade; nevertheless, she was glad to see Pat Neely. Emerging from the main cabin, Pat spotted her, called out, "Hi, Ara," and drew up to stand beside her.

Pat was several inches taller than Ara, and sturdily built. Her smile, the crinkles around her blue eyes, suggested an exuberance, a love of the outdoors. So did the careless way she had drawn back her wavy blond hair, wisps escaping from the loose tie and blowing in the wind.

"Alaska is lovely, isn't it? Bet this is your first trip here."

Ara told her that she had lived her entire life in a small town in Montana.

"I wouldn't live anywhere but here," Pat said. "The minute I got out of high school, I headed out to the wilderness miles and miles from Fairbanks. Before summer was over I had finished building myself a little cabin. I stayed out there alone for eight months."

Ara looked at her in amazement. "All alone?"

"It wasn't that bad," Pat said, laughing. "I did a lot of cross-country skiing, and I filled the evening hours with reading and my beadwork." She laughed again at Ara's sense of awe. "Everyone tried to talk me out of it—everyone, that is, except my uncle. Sam said, 'You go right ahead. When you get back, you'll know just who's in charge of your life.'"

Ara ventured dubiously, "How did you manage to survive the cold?"

"I cut plenty of wood and stored it in a safe, dry place. Being prepared, you know, is the key to all adventures. I have a sleeping bag that's good for minus sixty degrees. And you should have seen my clothes. My bunny boots."

"Bunny boots?"

Pat laughed again. "That's what they're called out here. Boots so thick and huge that there's no chance of getting frostbite."

Ara looked down at her sandals. "Sounds as if I could learn a lot about survival from you."

"It's nothing anyone can teach you. You have to learn that all on your own."

"Not everyone learns it," Ara commented. As she did thoughts of her father flitted through her mind. Could some unforeseen fate have befallen him, made it impossible for him to meet her? What if Sam Neely were dead? Out here, in this vast isolation, he might never be found.

"I've always liked Lone Port," Pat said, her enthusiastic voice interrupting Ara's private concerns. Pat was looking toward the weather-beaten houses that spotted the mountainside. "Curt and I just might settle here someday."

"I guess you're used to isolation," Ara replied, looking beyond where Pat gazed, toward the white tips of mountain peaks. "But I bet it gets miserable in the winter."

"Misery," Pat said, tapping her forehead, "is up here, not out there."

Ara looked at her curiously.

"Of course there's circumstances," Pat conceded. "Circumstances like whatever it is that's troubling you. Sometimes it helps to have someone to talk to. I've always got an ear to lend."

For some reason—Ara hadn't talked about it to anyone else—Ara found herself telling Pat about her mother's lingering illness and death.

The girl listened sympathetically. "I come from a small family, too," Pat said. "My folks were killed at sea when I was fourteen. All that's left is my uncle, Sam Neely, and me." She chuckled. "We get along like a dream. Curt and I run the shipping part of the company for him when he's gone, and he's up and gone a lot."

Pat believed she was Sam's only living relative—natural heir to his fortune. By the affectionate way she spoke of him, Ara realized she must consider him a father. She wondered what Pat would think if she told her Sam Neely had a daughter and that that daughter was talking to her now.

Ara didn't tell Pat all of what was on her mind.

"I sometimes believe I'm too much like my uncle. Sam travels all over," Pat said with pride. "He belongs to no one and to everyone, if you know what I mean." Pat leaned on the boat railing. "Do you read Robert Service? He has a poem, 'The Men that Don't Fit In.' In the silence they could hear the gurgle of water around the boat. " 'There's a race of men that don't fit in,' " she quoted, " 'a race that can't stay still; so they break the hearts of kith and kin, and they roam the world at will.' "

Yes, those lines did describe him, Ara thought bitterly. Sam Neely had broken her mother's heart when he had left Montana never to contact her again.

''There's more to Sam Neely than that,'' Pat declared, as if taking note of Ara's critical silence. ''Sam's a seeker. You of all people ought to understand. You're one of them, too, aren't you? A searcher? I knew that the moment I saw you.'' Pat slanted Ara a quick glance. Her expression made Ara think of Marc—of her feeling that they were two comrades meeting in some forlorn spot. Pat laughed. ''One kindred spirit always recognizes another.''

Ara's eyes fell to Pat's engagement ring. ''Speaking of kindred spirits, when's the big day?''

Pat fell silent, as if this were a subject she would rather avoid. After a while she said, ''Soon. Curt's been so insistent. So I've agreed to marry him the minute we dock in Kotzebue.''

But Curt had definitely told Ara that their wedding plans were on hold until Pat knew Sam Neely was safe. Pat might have heard from him; that was the only logical reason for her to change her mind.

Ara stared at her. Sam Neely was either hidden away on board the *Sea Rogue* or he had found some other way to contact Pat. Ara did not know why the news of their communication worried rather than relieved her.

Moreover, if Ara was any judge, Pat did not seem in the least enthusiastic over her fast-approaching wedding.

''Curt is really good-looking,'' Ara commented.

"Oh, yes, and just filled with ambition. Curt loves me dearly, understands me, too. In spite of that, I'm having second thoughts. Maybe I'm just not cut out for family life."

Ara studied her. Pat's attractiveness didn't spring from good looks, although she was attractive, but from a free spirit, an elusiveness that men were sure to find spellbinding.

Pat's quick laugh no longer had any ring of joy. "When I think of weddings, I can't help thinking of prisons. Anyway, the closer I get to Kotzebue, the more scared I get."

"You shouldn't marry him if you feel like that," Ara said. "Just wait until you're sure. I've always been told that when the right man comes along, nothing on earth will be able to keep you apart."

Pat's shrug had an unsureness about it, as if she were standing at an airplane door, waiting, parachute on, but not at all wanting to jump. "What if I never know for sure? You can see for yourself that Curt's quite the catch. He's not going to wait for me forever."

Ara made no reply.

"Curt and I get along well," Pat said, as if trying to convince herself. "And Sam likes him. He hired Curt several years ago to run the Kotzebue office. And Curt loves the challenge." She stopped short, her voice growing grave. "But I can't help thinking that the same thing might be happening to us that happened to Marc and me."

Marc's name linked with Pat's struck Ara like a slap in the face. "Marc and you?" she echoed.

"Yes, Marc. He's beautiful, isn't he? I mean, you could look all over the world and never find another man like him."

Ara hesitated, then tried to go on matter-of-factly. "What did happen to you two?"

"Not wanting to go through with the marriage was Marc's decision more than mine. He's like me, you know, only worse. He's the one who got cold feet. So we just up and called it off. To everyone's surprise. Sam was really disappointed. He wanted more than anything else for Marc and I to be a team. Mainly because of the business."

Ara felt an increased sense of shock. "I didn't know Marc and Sam were business partners."

"They are. You can go to the bank with that! Last year Marc threw in with Sam and became a part of Sam's Wayfarer Charter Company. Marc is in charge of the planes, while Sam manages the boats." She paused, then added fondly, "For some reason this old relic, the *Sea Rogue,* is Sam's favorite."

Ara felt a flare of cold anger. She tried to stifle it by telling herself that Marc had not actually lied to her. But he had—purposely—left information out, had failed to tell her Sam Neely and he were business associates.

"Sometimes I think Sam depends too much on Curt and me to run his shipping business." Pat's hands fell abruptly from the railing. "Well, I'd best be off. I'm headed into Lone Port again to meet Curt and do some shopping before the trading post closes. The Athabas-cans do excellent beadwork. Do you want to come along with us?''

''No, thanks,'' Ara said, feeling much worse for having talked to Pat. ''I'll just stay here on board.''

Ever since Ara had returned to the *Sea Rogue,* she had been convinced that someone had been watching her. She told herself now that Marc had followed her back on board and was merely keeping an eye on her; why, she couldn't even venture a guess. But no, there was more to it than that. The feeling of eyes on her was dark and scary.

Not even in the privacy of her quarters did she find comfort. Ara glanced uneasily about. The cramped space of Ara's cabin looked shrunken and warped. Two iron cots, separated by barely enough space to walk, were covered by hard mattresses and bedding as gray as the walls. Her eyes moved from spot to spot. It was almost as if she sensed that someone had been inside the cabin during her absence. She looked around, but could find nothing out of place. Of course, there was little to disturb; Ara had left nothing inside the room but her duffel bag.

As Ara opened her pack, she took note of the slight rearrangement of clothing. She had begun sorting through jeans, T-shirts, and shampoo, and shower items, when it suddenly struck her. Frowning, she looked through the contents of her bag again, then dumped everything out on the cot. Her suspicions were right. Her new 35-millimeter camera was missing!

Ara was certain she had put it back in her bag before leaving with Marc for Lone Port. A vision of Hal Bruins staring at the camera during their tense encounter in the cargo hold flashed through her mind. Ara was convinced Hal Bruins had been here in her room, had been the one who had rummaged through her personal effects in search of this item.

Had he somehow managed to break in, or did he have a key to her cabin? Confronting Bruins would serve no purpose, for he would only lie and say she had lost or misplaced the camera herself. Even though she knew this wasn't true, she had no way to prove its loss to be the result of deliberate theft.

It wasn't so much the loss of the camera that bothered her, but the reason behind Hal Bruins's taking it. The answer must lie in the cargo hold, beyond that sign that said NO ADMITTANCE. What was down in the lower level of the ship that Hal Bruins was afraid Ara might photograph?

Ara did not know whether the man she had followed down those steps had been her father or not. But whoever he was, he had gone to great lengths to avoid her. She must do everything she could to locate him.

Ara could not risk going back down there now. She would have to wait until darkness fell; then she would investigate. But she had a long wait ahead of her.

After placing her flashlight on the nearby stand, Ara, remaining fully dressed, stretched out on a cot.

She tried to relax, but a terrible tenseness tightened every muscle.

Marc had actually tried to force her into returning to Anchorage. She wondered why; she wondered even more about the worry—or was it anger?—she had detected in his features. She kept hearing Marc's voice calling after her, ''You'll be making a big mistake.''

Marc must know exactly what was going on aboard this ship. Because he was doing nothing about it, the thought frightened her. As she shifted her position, trying get comfortable, a strange thought flashed through her mind: what if the man she had seen today had been Sam Neely? What if her father himself was on board the *Sea Rogue*? If so, Marc and he must be mixed up in whatever crooked dealings were going on aboard the ship.

An annoying light intruded from the high porthole windows and kept her wide-awake. Almost one A.M. and it still seemed like midafternoon. How long would Ara have to wait for darkness?

Exhausted, she closed her eyes and tried to rest. When she opened them again, the few hours of nightfall had at last arrived, leaving the tiny cabin pitch-black, shadowless.

Taking up the flashlight, Ara slipped from her cabin. She had grown accustomed to the constant movement of ship and water. She was greeted only by an immense stillness, as if the ancient craft had been permanently grounded and left abandoned.

Ara increased her pace through the dim corridor,

through the empty dining room, and out into the cold, motionless air.

The deck, lit by a ghostly gleam from a solitary light, was overhung with quietness. Ara, flashlight remaining off, started toward the door marked NO ADMITTANCE. She was stopped by a clear, sharp sound that drifted to her from the middle of the forecastle. The clump, as if some heavy object had dropped from above, rang out startlingly loud. The noise was followed by a voice, hushed but angry. Ara could not make out what was said, but somehow she knew the speaker was Hal Bruins.

She drew forward, remaining out of sight against the dining room wall. She listened alertly, but the words were too indistinct and muffled to make out.

Ara drew in her breath and ventured a look around the side. The hatch leading to the lower level was open. A movable boom was set above it. Two men were working to reattach a large crate to the gooseneck fitting at the end of the winch. Hal Bruins, intent on his instructions, remained unaware of her watching them.

The crate was again hoisted, this time to the ship's edge, no doubt to be let down to a waiting boat.

Ara felt a chill settle over her. With all the hours of daylight, why would they choose one of the three hours of midsummer darkness to unload their cargo? There could be only one answer to that—whatever they were transporting inside that crate was illegal.

Ara thought of going for help. But even if time permitted, there was no one on board she could trust. She must act entirely on her own, and without benefit of her camera. Even though it was a great risk, she must get a glimpse of the second boat, so she would be able to identify it for the police.

She waited until all three men had left the *Sea Rogue*; then she slipped away from her place of concealment. She moved cautiously to the side of the deck.

A dim light played upon the water, fell across the dusky boat. Her gaze locked on the small vessel, a simple fishing boat, more battered even than the *Sea Rogue.* She frantically looked for some way to identify it, but how? There must be hundreds of small boats exactly like it, its color a dreary, nondescript charcoal, which blended with the murky sea.

She could make out several crates already loaded. The one just removed from the deck must have been the last of their cargo, for the three men made no move toward the *Sea Rogue* after placing it beside the others.

Voices carried up to her. She could not make out any sentences. She could only catch fragments of words—*plane . . . Anchorage.*

Ara ventured another look over the edge. She had not expected to see Hal Bruins directly below her. Just as Ara glanced down, Hal looked up. It was too late to try to hide; he had already seen her.

If she hadn't made a ''big mistake'' by returning to the *Sea Rogue,* she had made one now. Hal Bruins knew she had witnessed the removal of illegal cargo.

Fully alerted, he seemed to freeze for an instant;

then he swung around toward the walkway as if it were his intention to catch up with her.

Ara, like Bruins, remained immobile for a few moments; then she whirled and raced back to her cabin. Her hands, shaking a little, fumbled with the lock on the door. She shrank back into the room, listening breathlessly for the sound of his steps in the corridor.

Time passed. To Ara's surprise, no one tried to break through the door; no key turned in the lock. An awful silence hung around her; in spite of it, Ara could feel undercurrents of danger. Hal Bruins, or whoever he was working for, seemed only to be biding time, waiting for exactly the right opportunity to strike out.

Chapter Five

The storm hit when they were a few hours out of Lone Port. Starting with a simple gale, the wind soon mounted, hurling sprays of seawater across the deck. The old craft plowed onward, rocking and creaking against the churning break of waves.

Neither Pat nor Marc, who sat as if rooted to their seats in front of their morning meal, took the least bit of notice. Ara held on to her tin plate with one hand, keeping the other one solidly braced. If the table and benches hadn't been bolted to the plank floor, they would have slid across the room with the last alarming jolt.

"Hear you didn't do all that well in the race this year," Pat was saying to Marc.

Marc's smile showed that he accepted her statement as an observation, not as a criticism. "Team's getting old,'' he told her. ''They just don't have the stamina they used to. Tok led this race on heart alone.''

''Maybe it's time to retire them,'' Pat suggested.

''Tok wants to run, same as me. As long as he can, we'll strike out together, win or lose.''

Their conversation, the easy give and take of pals who often talked together, continued, their voices merging with the agitated blasts from outside.

''When will Freya have her pups?''

''I hope while I'm in Nome.''

The rocking beneath Ara's feet grew worse. She glanced worriedly from the window out at a raging sea filled with froth and foam.

Mark and Pat, as if they were spending a quiet Sunday afternoon in the park, kept on with their discussion of the Iditarod race.

''Maybe I'll just retire, too, the same time Tok does,'' Marc was saying. ''Every year the trail gets longer and rougher.''

''And the mountain ranges get higher,'' Pat tossed in.

''And the Yukon River gets wilder,'' Marc added, not to be outdone. He turned to Ara. ''Want some jelly for your toast?''

Ara accepted one of the small containers from the wire basket he extended. Grape. Upon reading the word, she felt a tightness grip her throat.

She hadn't touched her breakfast. Because Marc was watching her, Ara spread the toast with jelly. Then with great determination she brought a fork to her egg. It appeared to swim before her eyes, to be bubbling in a sea of grease. A queasiness struck the pit of her stomach.

"You look a little green, mate," Hal Bruins spoke up. He had just entered through the back corridor, wearing a long, black raincoat dripping with moisture. "What's the matter?" he continued tauntingly. "Haven't got your sea legs yet?"

Ara made an attempt to meet Hal's gaze, but his features began a dizzying spin.

"I've just spoken with the captain," Hal said, moving slowly forward and leaning back against the counter. The way he spoke the word *captain* seemed to be a put-down rather than a tag of respect. "I suggested that we anchor down and wait out the storm, but the old man is keen on riding it out."

Hal's pale eyes, unpleasantly bold, locked on Ara again. He walked around the counter, sniggering as he tossed her a paper sack. "Barf bag," he said.

Hal's words caused Pat and Marc to turn their full attention to Ara, attention she didn't in the least want.

"You're getting seasick," Marc said with disbelief. He took the plate from her. "You certainly don't want to eat this."

As Marc got to his feet, the boat lurched upward, rising and falling, hitting the water with a smack. Marc, in an adept maneuver, kept his balance and made his way to the cupboards.

With a look of concern he returned to Ara, placing a pack of crackers in front of her. "Eat as many of these as you can."

"That's just not going to do it," Pat declared, jumping to her feet. "Hang in there, Ara. I've got some pills in my room that will take care of the nausea."

Pat soon returned, forcing the pills on her and standing by with a glass of water. After the pills were down, all three of them continued to watch her expectantly.

Ara brought a cracker to her lips. The stale moistness made her want to choke. She forced herself to swallow, feeling more ill than ever.

Pat patted her shoulder solicitously, while Marc offered her another cracker. In the background Hal smirked as if enjoying her misery.

A loud, clear voice sounded over the intercom. "Would Hal Bruins and Marc Stewart report to the pilothouse." Static followed; then the words were repeated over the clattering noises of the storm.

Hal headed to the inside stairway leading to the top cabin.

"Curt's probably already up there," Pat said. "I'm going, too. Come on, Ara."

Once Ara rose, the room began whirling. Ara held on to the bench. When she at last felt able to start toward the stairs, she found herself staggering. Marc caught her and led her to a lounge beside the windows.

Not wanting him to know how ill she felt, Ara attempted a smile. "You go on, Marc."

"No, I'll stay here with you."

"I'll be fine. I just need to go back to my cabin and lie down for a while." When Marc still hesitated, she urged, "You had better check with the captain and see why he called for you."

''Right now you're as safe here as anywhere on the ship,'' Marc agreed finally.

''I'll come up as soon as I feel a little better.''

At the door Marc stopped again. ''If you do decide to join us on the upper level,'' he cautioned, ''be sure you use this stairway. Don't go out on the deck.''

Marc waited for a while, hand on the door latch. His sharp frown made him look very concerned. Ara was tempted to tell him just what she had witnessed last night. In fact, she almost did, and would have were it not for some internal last-minute warning. She knew nothing at all about him. And Marc had been careful to keep it that way, not even telling her that he was a business associate of her father's. Marc could very well be a part of . . . of what? The illegal running of whiskey, of weapons?

Ara watched silently as her opportunity to confide in Marc quickly passed. ''I'll be back as soon as I can,'' Marc said before he headed to the upper level.

After he left, Ara was glad that she had told him nothing. Her first plan was by far the sounder one. Just as soon as the storm passed and Captain Riggs was free, she would discuss the whole matter with him. After all, Farley Riggs was the only one she could be sure was *not* involved in whatever it was that was going on. If he were, Hal Bruins and his helpers would not find it necessary to unload cargo in the dead of night.

Ara stretched out on the lounge and closed her eyes, trying to ignore the sickening motions of the boat. Those pills Pat had given her were making her feel much worse. Or could that even be possible? Probably they hadn't even had time to take effect yet one way or another.

A half hour must have passed, and Marc did not return; neither did the storm show any signs of abating. Weakness made her feel shaky, and she had begun to sweat as if the medicine had induced some intense fever.

She thought of her father and wished he were here. In some sort of a dream state she imagined that he was in the room with her. He was telling her that he intended to take some action against the criminals who had taken over his boat.

After a while Ara's cloudy thoughts began to clear. Her stomach had settled a little. She slowly brought her feet to the floor. Hanging on to the wooden arm of the lounge, she was able to stand up, grateful that the spinning did not recur.

She was sure she could make it to the upper deck now. Weaving a little, she crossed to the stairway door. She was surprised when it stuck fast as she attempted to turn the latch. Somehow it must have locked when Marc had closed it.

Ara looked from the window to the rainswept deck. Feeling a desperate need for fresh air, she was not deterred by the stormy scene. Despite Marc's warning, if she were to join the others, she would have to take the outside steps up to the next level.

A spray of icy water caught her just as she stepped outside. Washes of sea had caused deep pools to remain on the floor of the deck. She did not even try to avoid them; instead she hurried forward, staying as close as she could to the cabin. The boat swayed and tipped a little portside. In spite of her efforts, she lost her handhold on the wall, and her unsteady steps careened out across the deck.

Wind gusted around her. Ara had not taken into account the terrible force of the gale. Propelled forward by it, she clutched the railing with both hands.

Because of her physical weakness, walking without anything at all to hold on to seemed almost an impossibility. But she must again cross the wide, clear area of the deck. She let go of the railing and began a frenzied attempt to reach the cabin wall.

Before she had taken more than a few steps, a vicious blow struck her. A searing pain cut across her shoulders, immobilizing her. The choppy waves, the heaving boat, darkened before her eyes. Ara reeled forward, falling, sliding.

Suddenly, as if she were being impelled by some force from behind her, some force other than the wind, she felt herself being hurled over the side of the boat. Before she had time to even draw a breath, she felt herself plunging deep down toward the violently swirling sea.

Chapter Six

The force of a striking wave at the exact moment of her fall slammed Ara back in toward the rough, slick metal of the boat. She reached out blindly, desperately. Her grasping hands just managed to catch hold of something solid. She hung on for dear life, blind and dazed by the stabbing pain between her shoulder blades, the burning of her palms, the icy water that totally drenched her hair and clothing.

Ara cried out for help, all the while knowing her voice would be drowned out by the howling of the wind, knowing one false move would hasten her plummet into freezing water and to almost certain death.

Keeping her eyes averted, not daring to look down at the churning, angry sea below, Ara carefully shifted her weight, trying to gain a firmer hold. Steadied, she realized that what had saved her was a metal ladder that hung over the side of the ship leading to the canvas-covered lifeboat lashed to the side.

She was hanging on at the ladder's end, feet dangling, supported only by her hands. Even though it seemed impossible, she must try to pull herself upward, to get some foothold.

Before she could bring herself to let go with one hand, another fierce wave struck her. The violent impact left her choked and gasping for breath. The frigid water knotted her muscles, made them feel numb and useless.

An agonizing pressure gripped her chest. She fought against panic. She wasn't going to be able to hold on much longer. She must quickly make use of what little strength she had left.

It was risky to let one hand bear the entire weight of her body. But she could not think of that. She had no choice but to make the attempt. She released her fingers from the iron railing. Without any direction from her, her hand snaked upward and locked on the rung above.

Groggy with pain, using every bit of strength she could muster, Ara pulled herself upward. She repeated the effort, this time battling against an overpowering weakness. At last both feet were solidly on the ladder!

Firmly braced, she now allowed herself to stop, to catch her breath. Then she began again the relentless climb upward. The worst lay just ahead of her. How was she ever going to get from the ladder back to the deck?

Half-blinded by the whipping wind, sick and jolted

from the swaying craft, Ara stopped again. She buried her head against her aching arm, wanting to give in to tears and defeat.

She would have to time her next action perfectly . . . wait for the wind to recede, then move swiftly. Without a handhold she must try to stand and reach for the deck's railing.

Ara tried once and failed, stepping down again and clutching the ladder, her whole body shaking. The second time, with one final burst of strength, she was able to catch hold of the railing and pull herself upward to the deck.

She did not try to stand for fear her knees would buckle from under her. She crawled across the open area and slumped against the ship's wall.

Ara had never felt so alone. The deserted deck, awash with sea spray, looked like a ghost ship. A strange other self had objectively stood by, directing her as she had hung between life and death; now this dimension had abandoned her. She was left on the verge of sobbing.

Her gaze moved to a heavy bar of wood that had slid across the plank floor to the ship's edge. Ara's fall had been no accident. Someone had used this bar as a weapon, had struck her with it. The great force of the blow had sent her hurtling forward to what was very nearly a horrible, drowning death.

She closed her eyes and thought of the announcement over the intercom, the locked door to the upper level. Had this all been a part of some conspiracy? She wondered now if she had ever actually been seasick. Pat could have slipped one of those pills into her coffee, pills used for the purpose of making her increasingly dizzy and weak.

At last Ara, soaked and shaking, managed to rise and open the door into the still-empty dining room. She slipped into the corridor and hurried toward her cabin. Once there, she couldn't stop the chattering of her teeth, the shivering. Ara climbed into the shower, where the tepid trickle of water brought some measure of warmth back into her chilled body. She dried her hair, wrapped herself in a robe, and lay huddled under a blanket on one of the cots.

She lay for hours trying to decide what to do. At last, overcome by the effects of shock and exhaustion, she fell into a strange, haunted slumber.

A soft knock on the cabin door awakened her. Marc's voice, sounding anxious, asked, ''Ara, are you in there?''

Ara sat up, head spinning, every muscle tense. ''Yes.''

''I got worried about you. Are you all right?''

''I'm fine. Or I will be after a while.''

Mare hesitated. ''Be sure and take a couple more of the pills Pat gave you.''

Gripped with apprehension, Ara waited without speaking.

''Is there anything I can bring you?''

''No. But thanks, Marc.''

During the long interval of stillness, Ara listened for the sound of his departing footsteps.

"Ara, I would like to talk to you." An edge had crept into Marc's voice. "I'm not very good at talking through closed doors."

She could picture how Marc would look, waiting patiently, blue eyes filled with concern. She felt herself longing to see him. In Marc's arms she would be safe, safe and comforted, just as she had been in Lone Port. But she could not rid herself of the warning. It encircled her, bright and strong, like the stern light on the *Sea Rouge*, and prevented her from making any move toward the door.

Before the attempt on her life, Marc had told her to use the stairway, the stairway that was mysteriously locked after he had gone through it to the upper level. Marc would know beyond all doubt that she would use the outside steps. Like it or not, Marc was the likely person to have been lying in wait for her out on that rainswept deck.

"I'll feel much better after I rest awhile," she told him.

Her words fell upon total silence. Ara held her breath. She had no doubt that Marc was still standing in the corridor, but she could not bring herself to speak again. After a while she heard his departing footsteps.

After that she didn't sleep. Regardless, early the next morning when she left her room, only the throbbing ache in her arms and shoulders told her that what had happened yesterday had been more than some terrible nightmare.

Sometime during the night the waters had grown calm and the ship had stopped its incessant rocking.

The sea now bore a calm, oily look, as unreal in placid calm as it had been in rage.

During her long hours of solitude, Ara had drawn some logical conclusions. If she could trust anyone, that person would be the ship's captain, Farley Riggs. If he had known about and approved the removal of the cargo, there would have been no necessity for Hal Bruins to have unloaded it in the dead of night. She would go to Captain Riggs with her story. He would be certain to take some action that would ensure her safe arrival in Nome.

Ara headed up the outside stairway that led to the top level. Farley Riggs was wandering around the bridge surveying the ship's damage. The long, weary siege at the wheel had not altered his appearance, so totally in control, so able to meet any conflict that might arise.

He stopped short when he saw her, his dark eyes growing cold and distant. But his words were friendly. "No wonder Sam sets this old relic up as his favorite. She glided through last night's storm like a real trooper."

The captain's appraising gaze settled on Ara. "Not so with you, I can see."

Ara took the opening his words left and told him all about her terrifying experience. The recounting made it all come back to her with sudden force, the shock of being hit from behind, of hanging on to the ladder with a death grip, of struggling against chilling wind and salt spray to avoid that perilous drop to the sea. He listened in his intent manner, making no comment at all, not even after she had finished with her story.

"Someone tried to kill me," she stated flatly.

After another long period of assessment, the captain answered, "You have just met these people. It's hard to believe that any of them would have a reason to . . ." He stopped again. "To push you overboard."

When Ara made no reply, his intent gaze became a challenge, which he was quick to cover up with a formal, businesslike air. "You say you were on the main level. Let's go down and take a look."

Farley Riggs led the way, hand sliding along the railing. Ara followed uncertainly. She hadn't expected her account of what had happened to her to be met with rejection, or, rather, with outright denial.

On the main deck, Ara walked over to the side, cringing a little as she peered down toward the iron ladder. Once again she felt the brutal force of the waves, the agony of her palms, still raw and burning, as she had tried frantically to cling to the iron rung.

"This is the place," she said, turning back to him.

As Farley Riggs paced around the deck, he stopped to lift the heavy wooden bar that had slid to a stop just beneath the railing. For a long time he studied the bar with the absorption he gave whatever his eyes fell upon. After a while he looked up to the top deck, then back at Ara. "Freak accidents happen during storms like the one we had last night."

"It wasn't an accident. I was deliberately attacked."

Farley Riggs pointed to the upper level. "There's a small hoist right above us. It's used for transport and is operated with a capstan bar. That's what this is. It's inserted in the capstan and used to turn a cable.''

''How did it get down here?''

''Whoever used it last must have left it in the capstan.'' He stared down at the wooden handle thoughtfully. ''Obviously the storm dislodged this bar and it fell and struck you.''

Ara's eyes met his, where they seemed to clash with his determined opposition. She was reminded of the fact that the captain himself had called for Marc and Hal Bruins to report to the wheelhouse during yesterday's storm. He was either in on the plot to kill her, or else she had misjudged his ability to analyze and interpret. ''I don't believe that's possible.''

''I'm not saying you received the full impact of this bar as it dropped from such a height. The blow would have been eased by wind currents. It would have—''

Ara cut off his words. ''This was no accident. I was struck across the back and knocked over the side.''

Nothing about him changed in the least, neither his reflective manner nor his grim, insistent stare. ''Many freak accidents occur during storms at sea.''

After a while the captain spoke again, one dark eyebrow arching. ''Why would you think anyone would want to harm you?''

If Farley Riggs was in on the scheme, he was already aware that she knew what was going on aboard his ship. She would gain nothing by not telling him. ''Hal Bruins and two other men waited until dark last night to unload cargo. I thought this was very suspicious, so I watched them. Hal Bruins spotted me, and soon afterward I had this *accident*. You can't tell me these two events are unrelated.'' She paused. ''I believe illegal cargo is being carried by this freighter.''

The captain turned away from her, then swung back. His slow words did not go along with his swift movement. ''You're wrong,'' he said. ''I know all about that cargo being unloaded. There was nothing illegal about it. In fact, I ordered the removal of those crates myself.'' Farley Riggs regarded her carefully. ''What happened to you last night was only an accident.'' His dark eyes, steely and cold with a warning or a threat, bore into hers. ''Just consider yourself very lucky. You could have been killed.''

A chill struck Ara. She was now thoroughly convinced. Whatever was going on aboard the *Sea Rogue,* the captain himself was a part of it.

Although Ara's body was stiff and sore, her spirits dampened, she no longer felt the queasiness in her stomach. After remaining seated in the dining room for a while, she became aware of pangs of hunger and realized it had been many, many hours since she had eaten.

She lifted the tin lid and helped herself to pancakes and sausage and poured herself a cup of steaming coffee. She returned to her table by the window, where she could look out at the sea.

''Mind if I join you?''

Curtis Carter, carrying a heaping plate of food, sat down across from her. He wore a white shirt that looked freshly laundered, contrasting with his long, straight dark hair. Unlike the others she had met this morning, he seemed gracious and pleasant. "Pat was telling me how sick you were yesterday. I'm glad you're feeling better."

She watched as Curt spread butter on his toast and slowly sampled it. His immaculate manners, as well as his dress, made him seem even more like an outsider, one not at home with rough seas and burly sailors. During her long hours of misery, she had not thought of Curt. Now she wondered why she hadn't gone to him with her story instead of Farley Riggs. Whether he believed her or not, he would give what she said his wholehearted consideration.

"I stayed upstairs with the captain all during the storm," Curt was saying.

Again she was impressed with his sense of responsibility.

Curt smiled. "I have to give Riggs credit; the old boy's a cool one. I can see now why Sam holds him in such high esteem."

"Did you help him with the operation of the ship?"

"Not really. I was just up there to supply support, to agree with his decisions and keep the coffee hot." He paused. "Did you enjoy the stop at Lone Port?"

"I didn't stay in town very long," Ara said. "I suppose Pat and you ate at Maureen's."

"I didn't even see Pat in Lone Port."

Ara frowned. She distinctly remembered Pat telling her she was meeting Curt in the village yesterday.

"In fact, I didn't see Pat until she came back on board. Lugging a bunch of packages." Curt smiled again. "How anyone could do all that shopping in Lone Port, I don't know. But it gives me some clue as to what I'm in for when we get married."

They ate awhile in silence. Once again it crossed Ara's mind that Curt and Pat were not well suited to each other. He was never going to understand her strong need for independence.

When she glanced up at him again, Curtis looked extremely serious. "I really expected Sam to show up at Lone Port. When he didn't, I began worrying about him myself. In fact, I just radioed the Coast Guard."

His sober eyes met hers. Ara felt her heart sink. Curt had some news about her father. She waited expectantly.

"The storm we had last night ran all the way up the coast. Sam's boat was found washed up along the shore near Nome."

Ara could not keep her voice level or steady. "What about Sam Neely? Have they found him?"

Curt's hazel eyes grew dark and somber. "It doesn't look at all good, Ara. His boat was empty."

Ara gazed out at the sea, darkened now, its deep gray full of secrets. Her father's boat had been found, but not his body. Had Sam Neely been washed overboard, or had he for some reason faked his own death?

Curtis's words kept coming back to her about Wayfarer Charters being in deep financial trouble. Her glimpse of a man aboard ship who looked like her father had been closely followed by the attack on her life. The two events suddenly seemed connected.

The captain might have been right—none of the people she had just met would have any reason at all to kill her. Not even Hal Bruins. Ara could testify to nothing. She had not set eyes on any contraband; she could not even describe the boat that had accepted the *Sea Rogue*'s suspicious cargo. Moreover, she could not supply the least bit of proof that an actual attempt had been made on her life. The police were not going to listen to mere theory and speculation, which was all she had to offer them.

No matter what was taking place on her father's ship, Ara felt certain of one fact: Sam Neely was not dead. Although the belief gave her a sense of relief, it also brought with it grave doubts of him and caused frightening questions to surface. Someone had tried to kill her last night, and who could be behind it all but the man who had invited her here?

Her father could have planned it all from the very beginning. Of course he would know all about the Londell money. If something happened to Ara, he, as her closest living heir, could lay claim to the sizable Londell fortune. A shudder passed over Ara. Had Sam Neely planned all along to lure her up here to Alaska to meet with a fatal accident upon the *Sea Rogue*?

Chapter Seven

The fog set an eerie cast over the port of Nome. Ara could barely make out the weatherworn buildings that spotted the bay. They had anchored just before the few hours of Alaskan darkness had settled over the town. She saw no sign of activity, just lone lights diffusing their scattered messages of human occupation.

Ara had not been able to sleep. Standing on the deck, she shivered a little from the cold. She was acutely aware of an immense silence, of a vast sense of space filled with endless valleys that somewhere in the remote, far-distant wilderness would join with mountain peaks.

A loneliness gripped her. She felt as if she had arrived here against her will, far away from all that was safe and familiar, alone in some other world.

A movement below her on the landing dock caught

her attention. A large form appeared to her through a haze of fog. A hushed voice carried by the wind called her name. ''Ara.''

Her heart leaped. Who else could it be but Sam Neely? When she had least expected to, she had found her father!

Although she wanted to race down the open landing door and into his arms, caution stopped her. Slowly her hands released their grip on the railing. Reluctantly she began to walk down the steel walkway that joined with the large dock. At the edge of it she stopped, leaving a wide space between them.

The two stared through the heavy mist as though they were each trying to gauge the other.

Where had he come from? Had he been on board all along, or had he been waiting at Nome for the *Sea Rogue* to arrive and anchor for the night?

Ara could not tell whether he was the man she had glimpsed aboard ship. But she had no doubt in her mind that this man was actually Sam Neely. At this close range, she would have recognized him anywhere from the picture her mother had given her. He looked like a man of action, as though he belonged to a stormy sea or to some remote battlefield. His black hair, ruffled and damp, curled around his broad face. His rugged beard was shot with gray. She couldn't help feeling wary of him, but only until his battered face relaxed into a smile.

''What do you say to a daughter you didn't know you had?''

Ara felt choked but attempted to be lighthearted. " 'Hello' would be fine."

"Hello, then." His smile remained. "You should have sent me your picture. I was looking for someone big and ugly like myself."

She did not return his smile, but became deadly serious. "Why didn't you board? This is your boat, or so they tell me."

He did not speak, just remained gazing at her.

"Pat and Curt have been worried sick about you. Curt thinks you've met with some terrible fate."

"That's exactly what I want everyone to think. For now. Did you tell anyone—Pat or Curtis—who you are?"

"I told Marc Stewart."

"You shouldn't have told anyone. Being associated with me will only place you in danger." He drew in a deep breath. "It was risky, my trying to contact you, but it was a risk I had to take." Gray eyes, accustomed to squinting, searched her face. "I had to see for myself that you are all right."

It flitted through Ara's mind to confide totally in him, to share with him her suspicions concerning the surreptitious unloading of cargo, concerning her miraculous escape from death. The desire to tell him flared, then died just as quickly. "Don't worry about me. I'll be fine."

His eyes left her face, skimming in an alert, watchful way the misty decks of the *Sea Rogue*. "I wish I could be sure of that."

"You're going to have to tell me just what's going on," Ara insisted.

Sam looked away from the boat out across the obscure, dark water. His manner left an impression of total absence from her, but Ara knew his thoughts centered on the danger that now involved them both.

He spoke at last. "I can't tell you what's going on, Ara. Because I don't know myself." He turned back to face her, brows knitted and the lines in his face tightening. "You're just going to have to trust me. You're going to have to do exactly what I tell you."

Ara did not reply.

His penetrating stare had about it an edge of challenge. "If you don't, you're liable to get dragged into a situation I won't be able to get you out of."

Ara's heart sank. She had found her father, but he was a common crook. He had instigated and was carrying out some rogue plot to save his company by faking his own death. And now she was caught right in the middle of it. Her only consolation was his apparent concern for her safety. Surely he couldn't be involved in the attack on her life—unless his show of caring, too, was only a carefully planned act.

Ara forced herself to say, as if she fully believed in his innocence, "You know as well as I do that something illegal is going on aboard the *Sea Rogue*. Surely you must have some idea what it is. And who's involved in it."

"I don't. But I'm doing all I can to find out. I had my suspicions before I sent for you, but I never imagined things would happen quite so fast. Believe me, I would never have knowingly put you in any danger.''

He sounded so sincere that Ara wished she could give him the benefit of the doubt. ''But I am involved now. And I need to know everything you can tell me. What do you know about Farley Riggs? The captain claims to have worked for you for a number of years. Can he be trusted?''

Sam hesitated. ''It's best for you not to trust anyone.''

If her father was telling the truth, then why was he acting this way, hiding out like some common criminal? If he were innocent of any wrongdoing, he was getting in way over his head. ''Why don't we just go to the police right now, with whatever information you have?'' Ara suggested. ''It would be much wiser to let them handle this.''

Sam shook his head. ''I don't have a scrap of evidence to turn over to the authorities.''

''But please. We can leave—''

He interrupted, his words determined and sharp. ''No, I have to handle this my way.''

My way—hadn't all of his dealings been his way? Clearly his every action had always been motivated by pure self-interest. Ara wondered just how far Sam Neely would be willing to go to protect himself and his secrets.

Sam's voice took on an air of command. ''Ara, I want you to leave this ship and catch the first flight out today. You must go back to Anchorage. I won't

allow you to do anything else. For your own good. I'll
contact you there just as soon as I can. You must—''

A flashlight flickered on from the deck just above
them. It had caught him unaware and he glanced up,
startled. The knowledge that someone else on the *Sea
Rogue* was wide-awake, that someone was likely to
spot them, caused Sam Neely to step back quickly.
Without another word he whirled from Ara and hurried away, blending into the darkness and the fog.

''Wait!''

Ara started after him. She was astounded that anyone could disappear so rapidly, so completely. He
could have slipped aboard one of the other boats, or
he could have headed into Nome. In any event, Ara
had a feeling she was not going to see Sam Neely
again until he wanted to be found.

By the time daylight streaked across the sky, the fog
had lifted, leaving in its wake a clean, sharp clearness.
Ara left her cabin and on the deck encountered Captain Riggs.

Whenever she saw him, she noticed first his immaculate clothing, his trim beard and mustache, iron
gray, rather than white. She drew closer, tightly gripping the duffel bag in her hand. His arched eyebrows,
his measured gaze, his thin lips that reposed in con-
templation before any speech escaped them, left an
image that contradicted that of the rough-and-tumble
sea captain who had guided them through yesterday's
storm.

''Good morning,'' he said with a quick, rather false

smile. He glanced down at her luggage. "Are you leaving us?"

"Yes. I've decided to stay in Nome for a while, then fly back to Anchorage."

"I don't blame you," he replied, as if she were some tourist he had met in passing and likely would never see again. "Everyone should experience Nome." He continued in a chatty manner that struck Ara as unusual for him. "Whenever I dock here, I can't help thinking of Captain Cook." His gaze wandered to the sea, then back to her. "Cook was one of the first people to map this region, you know."

"I'm not too familiar with the area's history," Ara said. "Actually all that comes to mind when I think of Nome is gold."

"Nome was once quite the boomtown," he replied. "But now more people think of it only as the finish line for the annual dogsled races."

"Does Wayfarer Charters have an office here?"

He hesitated. "Yes. But it's probably one of those times you'll find it locked." By the quick way he turned from her, she saw that he did not wish to go on with the subject. He started away, saying over his shoulder, "Enjoy your stay in Nome."

Their brief talk had made her even more uneasy, even more anxious to be leaving the *Sea Rogue* for good; nevertheless, she did want to say good-bye to the others, most of all to Marc.

Ara found Pat in the dining room lingering over a cup of coffee. She sat down beside her and told her that she was leaving. "I don't like bad news early in the morning,'' Pat said, looking genuinely disappointed. ''I was planning on your going with us to Kotzebue. I wanted you to be there when Curt and I exchange our vows.''

''I wish I could, but I have business I must see to.''

''Marc isn't going to like your leaving without even saying good-bye to him. I think he's quite taken with you. You might be walking out on the world's best opportunity.''

Pat's words caused Ara to blush like some silly schoolgirl. ''Do you know where I could find him?''

''No telling. Marc left the boat right after breakfast.''

Ara stood up, and Pat did also.

''Where will you be staying?''

''I'm going to get a room here in Nome for a day or two. Eventually I'll end up back in Anchorage. At Mountain View Resort.''

Pat nodded. ''I know the place. If I run across my uncle, I'll tell him where to find you.''

''I really do wish I could be at your wedding. You have my very best wishes.''

Pat looked saddened by their parting, but added brightly, ''Who knows? Maybe we'll meet on the same trail again someday.''

Ara, who had walked to the entrance, forced a cheerful little wave. ''Until then,'' she said. ''When you see Marc and Curt, tell them good-bye for me.''

Pat Neely's beaming face, her bright smile, had served to dispel Ara's suspicions of her. She left thinking that if they had lived in the same town in Montana, they would have ended up the best of friends.

She headed toward the landing deck. Although Ara was anxious to disembark from the old craft that had almost brought about her death, she still dreaded getting off in such a bleak, isolated place. She wondered how Nome would look in the winter months, covered in ice and snow. Would the locals ever grow accustomed to the Arctic breeze that even in June was causing her to chill?

She drew to a stop at the very spot where just last night she had talked with her father—if, indeed, he had been her father. She didn't know even where to begin her search for him.

Ara set down her duffel and stared out across the lonely Bering Sea, then toward Nome. An occasional sailor moved among the boats, burly forms clad in navy jackets, but otherwise the town seemed still asleep. Ara imagined what the little port must have been like during the gold-rush days, ships jamming the harbor, tents crowding the shoreline. Now it appeared occupied only by stragglers, by tough hangers-on from more prosperous years.

Only a short walk led from the rock wall that held back the sea to the main street of Nome. Ara set out at once, trying to convince herself that she wasn't just wasting time on useless efforts. She must find her father again. She would never be able just to walk away without knowing what sort of trouble he was facing.

"Ara."

She glanced around, her troubled thoughts receding

at the sight of Marc. He caught up with her in a few quick strides. Dampness mingling with rays of sunlight sparked a golden glimmer in his thick hair. He wore an old sea jacket that added a dimension of ruggedness to his features, ruggedness that vanished with his smile.

"Welcome to Nome." He took the duffel bag from her and slung it over his shoulder as he fell into step beside her. "The very name rings of adventure, doesn't it? Makes you want to start panning for gold!"

"Do you come here often?"

"I have a little cabin just outside of town."

They walked along an unpaved street, past wooden-frame houses that looked as though they had battled the elements and lost. So did the battered old trucks and four-wheel-drive vehicles parked in front of them.

"I didn't know Nome had a sea wall," Ara said.

"The Bering Sea can get very rough. Back in 1913, a storm blew in that tore the town to pieces, drove ships right through the main street. Nome never regained its former glory—most of the gold seekers gave up and went home."

"It seems a harsh place to live."

"During one storm, water flooded the graveyards and uprooted coffins." He cast her a quick glance, smiling at her reaction. "They don't bury people here in winter because of the permafrost. They wait until Memorial Day."

Suddenly Marc stopped walking and checked his watch. "Not much time for Nome this trip," he said.

"The *Sea Rogue* pulls anchor in less than an hour. And I've got lots of errands."

"I'm not getting back on the boat."

Marc set down the duffel. "Somehow I didn't think so. What are you going to do?"

"I plan to stay here for a few days."

She studied his face for some clue to his thoughts. His manner did not change in the least.

"Then I'd suggest you stay at the Gold Strike Hotel. It's only a block or so from here."

Ara felt a little disappointed by his quick acceptance of her decision. She had expected him to try either to convince her to return to the *Sea Rogue* or to catch a plane back to Anchorage.

"Let's take a little side trip," he said, steering her across the deeply rutted road. After a short walk, he caught her arm to stop her. "Here's what I wanted you to see."

Ara looked toward a thick, square structure of rough-hewn cement. The rusty iron door looked like the entrance to a gigantic safe. Even Ara would have had to duck to step inside it.

"This is a vault," Marc said, "where the Three Lucky Swedes stowed their gold. They made a strike here in 1898, and their mine paid off a million a year for seventeen years."

"What a find."

"It had its day, that's for sure. The Three Lucky Swedes' strike produced the third-largest gold nugget in the world, a hundred and eight ounces."

"Is gold still found here?"

"The big veins that are known about have all been depleted. Large companies still dredge, but its a costly operation. People still pan for gold along the bay and along the river. I even do a little prospecting myself. But all I've found so far are small flakes of gold. Nothing that's going to make me a millionaire."

"Is that your goal, to be rich?" Ara asked as they strolled on.

"No, my goal is to be happy."

For a brief moment, silently walking beside him, Ara herself felt a sudden rush of freedom, of happiness. But it faded long before they had reached the main street, which was just beginning to awaken to early morning activity.

"Here we are, the Gold Strike Hotel," Marc said. "Right on the Bering Sea. You'll enjoy the view."

Marc caught her hand. His grasp was warm and strong. Their eyes held, and Ara felt a protest rise in her heart against his leaving. He would run his errands and return to the *Sea Rogue*. The old freighter would chug on toward the Arctic Circle, and it would take Marc with it, take him far away from her.

"Good-bye, Marc."

His hand tightened around hers, then drew away. "Good-bye, Ara."

Marc left abruptly, his steps quick, his head held high, as he headed north. Once he reached the corner, he turned back and waved. He hadn't even bothered to ask how he might be able to contact her again.

Chapter Eight

Immediately after checking in, not knowing where to begin looking for her father, Ara stood in front of the hotel. Her sense of aloneness grew as she gazed down the unpaved street toward the intersection where Marc had turned back to wave at her.

She had been foolish to imagine that Marc was involved in the attack made on her life. He had been nothing but kind and supportive to her. If Marc had intended to harm her, he had passed up a perfect opportunity when they had been alone by that isolated river in Lone Port.

Now that Marc was gone and she might never see him again, Ara realized she should have trusted him.

Still uncertain of which way to go, she headed north, the direction Marc had taken. When Nome had been only a far-distant dot on the map to her, she had pictured it much differently. She had harbored vague notions that the place would resemble Cripple Creek, Colorado, or some of the other famous gold-rush towns she had visited. But nothing except the glitzy, Western-style hotel looked in any way commercialized. In fact, the buildings bore a bleak look, a barren starkness, probably a more authentic portrayal of life in remote places than what was normally displayed for tourists.

Ara passed stores and houses so bleached and weathered by the wind and elements that they looked as if paint would no longer cling to their wooden sides. After walking for a long time, on a side street she located her father's office. It faced the sea, a wooden structure with an old-fashioned facade, high and flat. Peeling black letters on the weatherworn front advertised WAYFARER CHARTERS.

Just as the captain had predicted, the door was shut and padlocked. Ara peered through the window into a small, drab room. Above a marred oak desk hung a yellowed calendar with pages curling upward. The only furniture other than the desk and chair consisted of a shabby-looking lounge and a coffee table with a half-filled ashtray. Like the *Sea Rogue*, the office seemed woefully neglected and out-of-date. If Ara didn't know better, she would think the business was permanently closed.

She lingered a moment outside the deserted building. The brisk Arctic wind whipped at Ara's hair and clothing as she made her way down to the waterfront.

Along the docks, among the boatmen, if anywhere, she might find news of her father.

Most of the boats tied up along shore were small fishing craft. Ara inquired of a group of young men unloading their morning's catch if they knew Sam Neely. "We are not from here," one of them hastily replied.

She walked on.

A muscle-bound fisherman at the end of the dock, face reddened by the sun and wind, stopped his work when confronted by her questions. A sadness crept into his eyes as he squinted toward her. "Haven't you heard?" He tried to break the news as carefully as he could. "Sam's boat washed in yesterday, or what was left of it. I saw it myself, damaged beyond repair. I don't know how it managed to stay afloat."

A sick apprehension gripped Ara as she once again pictured her father lost at sea, dead in a watery grave. Sam Neely might actually be dead, for all she knew. The man she had talked to so briefly last night might not have been her father at all, but some impostor.

"I wish I had better news for you," the fisherman said, "but from the looks of that boat, no one, not even Sam Neely, could have survived."

Her heart resisted the idea that she had not seen and talked to her father last night. He had the bearing she had expected and he had looked remarkably like the photograph she carried.

But if he were alive, could she trust him? He was the only person who had any reason to want her out of the way. If he inherited the Londell money, he would be able to save himself from financial ruin. But what kind of a man would be willing to murder his own daughter?

Surely not Sam Neely. If only she could find him, he would be able to explain exactly what was going on. He would tell her why he hiding, why he wanted to be presumed dead.

Deep in thought, Ara had totally forgotten about the sailor. He had gone back to work, making preparations to sail, but he turned back to say to her. "We'll all miss Sam. He was a good man, the best of the best."

Ara thanked him for his time and walked on.

Ara felt discouraged. If Sam was still alive, she was never going to find him. Still, she continued along the row of boats, stopping here and there to make inquiries.

At last Ara retraced her steps back toward Nome, pausing now and then to look out toward the sea.

"Miss." Ara turned around to find a white-haired man, lean and hollow-eyed, standing at the threshold of a rickety fishing boat. The word *Scamp*, lettered on the side, seemed a more fitting name for him than for the craft.

"My name's Ben Greer," he said as she stepped toward him. "I heard you asking around about Sam."

Ara's hopes rose. "Do you know anything about him?"

He glanced around as if he had information he wanted to keep secret, then motioned her to come aboard. Ara hesitated, then followed him inside the cabin, which was dark and oily and smelled of the sea.

"I overheard you talking to Clyde." He ran gnarled fingers though his hair and across his chin, which was in bad need of a shave. "I couldn't bring myself to let you leave like that. Sure, Sam's boat washed ashore, but he managed to survive."

"Are you sure? How do you know?"

"I talked to him just last night. He was right there." He pointed toward an empty captain's chair. "Sam had supper with me on my boat."

During the silence that followed, Ben Greer lifted a coffeepot from the stove and poured coffee into an old mug. Ara accepted politely, and he watched as she took a sip of the strong, bitter liquid.

He chuckled. "Sam says I make the best coffee he's ever drunk. Maybe too strong for the likes of you, though."

"No, the coffee's good," Ara replied.

"Sam was acting real strange last night," the old sailor went on. "After I gave him a bite to eat, I just out and asked him what was wrong. He swore someone was after him. Said I shouldn't tell anyone I had seen him." He grinned at Ara, the smile revealing gaps in his teeth. "I don't think he meant you. Old Sam's not one to be afraid of a pretty young slip of a girl."

"Did he tell you who was after him?"

"No, he wouldn't tell me nothin' else. I wanted him to stay on my boat. No one would ever find him here, but he wouldn't agree to that. Said he had important business to see to."

"Here in Nome?"

Ben Greer hesitated a moment, as if deliberating whether or not to betray his friend's confidence.

"Please tell me. I only want to help him. I—I'm his daughter."

Once again the gap-toothed smile lit his face. "That boy sure does keep a lot to himself. Didn't ever hear nothin' about any daughter."

"If you'll tell me where he is, I promise you I will keep the information to myself. I must find him, that's all. Whatever trouble he's in, I believe I will be able to help him."

He gave her a long, silent look, as if the thought of her being family gave him sympathy toward her. "Sam said he was going on up to that little Eskimo village. Kotzebue."

"Thank you," Ara said. "I can't tell you how much I appreciate your help."

Ben Greer walked with her to the entrance. "When you find Sam, don't tell him we had this talk. Remember, if Sam asks, you didn't hear a word from me."

Although Sam Neely would be no safer in Kotzebue than he would be here, Ara nevertheless felt a great sense of relief. Talking to Ben Greer had assured her that the man she had met last night was truly her father, and in a small, isolated village like Kotzebue must be, she should have little trouble finding him again.

With a firm plan and destination in mind, Ara hurried back to the hotel. Since the *Sea Rogue* had already left, she would call the airport for the next flight out.

Ara quickly dialed the number. "I'd like to take the next flight to Kotzebue," she told the ticket agent.

After a slight delay, a pleasant woman's voice told her, "Due to maintenance problems, the plane service to Kotzebue has been temporarily delayed."

"When is the next flight out?"

"The next flight is Thursday at three P.M."

No plane would be leaving Nome and heading north for three days. Ara's hopes quickly deflated. She was forced to stay in this dismal place. By the time she arrived in Kotzebue on Thursday, her father would already be gone.

At noon, sunk in gloom and frustration, Ara went down to the hotel dining room. She glanced at the menu, the prices of the food momentarily taking her mind off of her troubles. She had never paid ten dollars for a hamburger before, or two dollars for a cup of coffee.

While waiting for her food to arrive, Ara gazed out the window across the Bering Sea. Strange to think that she was seated here only one hundred and sixty miles from Russia. She was closer to Russia than to Kotzebue.

Ara was beginning to think that getting off of the *Sea Rogue,* which had sailed hours ago, was another of her many mistakes. At least on the ship she had been moving. Now she was stuck, waiting in this forsaken little town for Thursday's flight.

"How do you like the ten-dollar special?" Ara's heart leaped at the sound of a familiar voice.

She looked from the gray of sea into the sparkling blue of Marc's eyes. Her spirits lifted, and she felt a little catch in her breath as she answered, ''Back in Montana I could buy a thick steak for the same price.''

''Everything has to be shipped in here. That causes the prices to skyrocket.'' Marc seated himself in the bench across from her, calling, ''Nellie, would you bring me a hamburger and coffee, too?''

''Why aren't you aboard the *Sea Rogue*?'' Ara asked.

''I missed the boat.'' He smiled at her. ''I told you I had a lot of errands to run.''

He hadn't really missed the *Sea Rogue*'s departure. Ara was touched by his obvious plan to remain in Nome because of her, and she found all of the suspicions she had harbored concerning him falling away. She openly admitted to herself how glad she was to see him.

''Are you still planning to go to Kotzebue?''

Marc nodded. ''I'm taking the Cessna. I'm leaving first thing in the morning.''

Ara did not hesitate. ''Will you take me with you?''

''I will take you to the airport so you can go back to Anchorage.''

''Thanks for nothing. I'll get to Kotzebue on my own.''

Marc studied her, lips set in challenge. Then, as if he were acknowledging his inability to change her plans, his expression softened. A hint of amusement came into his eyes. ''Maybe we can strike up some kind of a deal.''

"What are the terms?"

He slanted her a considering look. "You can fly with me to Kotzebue in the morning—but only if you agree to spend the rest of the day with me. I have some last-minute business here, and you can be my assistant."

Her time in Nome no longer stretched before her like some long, dreary sentence. She smiled at Marc and said, "Fair enough."

Chapter Nine

Once in Marc's truck bouncing over an endlessly long and empty patch of beach road, Ara asked, "During the storm, after the captain sent for you, did you stay in the wheelhouse?"

Marc, surprised by the question or by the accusing tone Ara could not quite drive from her voice, answered promptly, "Yes."

"What about the others?"

"Hal left right away for the engine room. Pat, as usual, sprinted off, no one knows where, which sent Curt into a dither. Curt spent most of his time looking for her."

"What about Captain Riggs?"

"He never left and neither did I. Why do you ask?"

"I was just curious, wondering why the captain had

called for you when you're not a member of the crew.''

''The answer to that is simple. Farley needed all the help he could get. Besides, I am part of the company.''

A fact, Ara thought, that Marc for a very long time had neglected to tell her. Ara continued to study him. She should have avoided being alone with Marc, yet here she was on this isolated shoreline headed far away from Nome . . . to where?

''Why are you looking at me like that, Ara? And why all the questions? Are you still believing that you saw Sam on board the *Sea Rogue?*'' His brows raised critically. ''I suppose you think that one of us smuggled him on board and was deliberately hiding him.''

''Why would Sam Neely have to hide? Just what kind of trouble is he in?''

Marc's gaze left the road and strayed, not toward her, but toward the great stretch of tundra that, far in the distance, began to roll and rise. ''Why do you ask me?''

Earlier Ara had considered telling Marc about the attempt made on her life, but now she decided against it. Either Marc already knew about it, or he would, if he thought she was in such grave danger, refuse to take her on to Kotzebue. In any event, Ara couldn't risk confiding in him, not about that or about the brief meeting she had had last night with her father. ''Who else could I ask?''

''The logical person would be Sam himself.''

''Then you must believe he's still alive.''

Marc didn't reply. Ara couldn't understand his refusal to discuss Sam Neely with her, but she did know that no amount of persuasion was going to bring that about. The stillness, the closed look on Marc's face, increased her worries concerning her father.

"If Sam is in serious trouble," Marc finally said, "it may spill over to you. That's why I don't want you to go to Kotzebue. I'm only allowing it because I know you will go regardless of what I say or do."

In the silence that followed Ara could hear the wind whipping around the cab. Sudden gusts sent waves lapping across the sand close to the makeshift road. She cast an uneasy look over her shoulder, where the distant outline of Nome had grown small and indistinct.

"Where are we going?"

"I have to take supplies out to my cabin. It's not far now. In fact, it's just over the next rise."

He had no sooner spoken than a rustic wooden structure came into view. An old dog, lounging beside a huge stack of firewood, rose and watched alertly as they approached.

As Marc switched off the engine, the dog sprang forward.

"Tok," Marc said, bounding as happily toward the dog as the dog did toward him.

Cold wind blasted Ara as she opened the door. Wrapping her arms close to her heavy T-shirt, she walked toward them.

"Ara, meet Tok, my lead dog." Marc patted the

heavy fur with its distinctive dark markings. "We've run many a race together, old Tok and I."

For such a strong, enlivened animal, Tok had a gentle, obedient manner that spoke of keen intelligence. "Does he bite?"

"Not unless he thinks someone's a threat to me," Marc replied, slanting Ara a teasing look. "He's not real sure of you. You're not a danger to me, are you, Ara?"

It was more likely to be the other way around, Ara thought. Yet Marc seemed reassuringly innocent as he knelt by the dog's side.

Ara petted the dog, her hand moving close to Marc's. "He has lovely eyes. In fact, he is beautiful."

Marc laughed. "Don't know if old Tok would approve of being called beautiful, but the blue eye color is the mark of a purebred Siberian husky, one of the best sled dogs. Some people run malamutes or Samoyeds, but all of my team are huskies. Come on, I'll show you the rest of the dogs." Seeing her shivering, he changed his mind. "No, first, we had better find you a parka."

As they entered the cabin, Ara's gaze fell to the large stone fireplace, and she longed for a blazing fire. The comfortable room, the thick rug in front of the hearth, the large shelves crammed with books, all seemed to fit in with her own image of Marc.

He came to stand beside her. Ara felt an intense awareness of him, could smell the scent of wood smoke and pine that clung to his jacket. He reached for her hand, and his warm touch sent a thrill through her.

She stepped away. "I love your cabin," she said. "But I can't imagine being snowed in out here."

"It's OK," he answered, smiling. "That is, if you're with the right person."

He drew closer, and Ara felt the gentle pressure of his arms around her. "You make me wish it were snowing now."

Ara, as if it were the most natural thing in the world, snuggled close against him. She found herself responding to his kiss more fully, more passionately, than she had the first time. For a moment there were only the two of them in the entire world, lost in the rapture of being alone together.

A sudden tap upon the door made them break self-consciously apart. "Come in," Marc called.

A feeling of disappointment, and yet a measure of relief, filled Ara as a short, dark man wearing small sunglasses stepped inside the cabin. "Welcome back, Marc," he greeted.

His sudden appearance had startled Ara, but Marc seemed unsurprised. "Ara, this is Emil Akmulik. He's my next-door neighbor, even though out here next doors are miles and miles apart. He takes care of my place while I'm away. He looks after my nine dogs."

Emil grinned broadly. "Correction, Marc. Sixteen."

"What? Freya's had her pups?"

"Seven of them," Emil announced proudly. "Just thought I'd stop by and tell you the news."

"Let's go take a look."

Marc selected a wrap from the closet. Although Ara had always thought of parkas as designed for ice and snow, the one she slipped on was lightweight like one of the windbreakers she had back home. The material was pale blue decorated with beautiful geometric designs sewn on by hand.

Emil left them at the doorway. "I'd like to join you, but I'm on my way to town," he explained, and set out on foot.

Excited, high-pitched barking greeted them as they walked around the building. Because Ara had reservations concerning Marc and the intimate moment they had just shared, the pups served as a welcome distraction.

Inside the wire fence the proud mother was surrounded by active, yipping pups, their eyes barely opened, their small legs still clumsy.

"My new sled team has arrived!" Marc opened the wire cage door, reached inside, and handed Ara a squirming pup, then took one for himself.

The small pup Ara held in her arms had soft, fuzzy fur and raccoonlike black markings around his eyes. "He's adorable."

"They may someday place in the Iditarod. With lots of time and training, of course."

"The race sounds exciting." Ara stroked the puppy's soft fur. It was difficult to imagine the tiny creature in her arms growing big enough to help pull a sled. The pup nuzzled her with his little black nose, then snuggled into the warmth of her jacket.

"Over a thousand miles, one hundred and fifty of

them along the Yukon River. It's held in April because in summer the land becomes spongy, in places like a swamp. But, yes, it is exciting—man against time and the elements.''

"Do you enter every year?"

"Only for the pure fun of it. Someday, though, I might win the jackpot.'' He smiled engagingly. "That's everyone's dream, isn't it?"

Ara hated to give her puppy up, but knew he needed to go back with his mother. Marc took him from her and carefully placed both puppies alongside Freya so they could nurse.

In a pen set a distance away from the others, Ara noticed a large dog that looked different from the rest. It crouched in the corner, yellowish eyes wild and glaring. "That isn't a dog—it's a wolf," Ara cried.

"A black wolf. They are hunted here in Alaska for their magnificent pelts. This one has a strange history. Pat found him caught in a trap just north of here where the wooded area begins. And what does she do?'' He went on, an affectionate tone in his voice. "Pat makes me go out and bring him here to nurse back to health.''

"Pat is very kind, isn't she?"

"No animal should have to suffer like that.'' A muscle worked in Marc's jaw. "He had pulled and chewed so hard, he very nearly lost his leg. Even if he had gotten free, he wouldn't have survived a week in the wilderness.''

"What will you do with him?"

Marc paused. "Turn him loose, when the time comes.''

The animal raised his head, eyes intently following Ara's movement as she stepped as close to the cage as she dared.

"He's so wild. Aren't you afraid he will turn on you?"

"Animals are smarter than people give them credit for. He knew I was trying to help. Unlike people, they know who their friends are—and their enemies. Wolves have a bad reputation, one they don't really deserve. They're a lot like dogs. If raised as pups and treated kindly, they make loyal pets. But this fellow, he'll never be tame. He belongs to the wilderness."

Marc stood very straight and still. "Just like Pat," he said.

Again Ara could not help but interpret the undercurrent of deep affection that came into his voice whenever he spoke of Pat. Ara felt a tinge of annoyance and hated to admit to herself that this feeling sprang from jealousy. She wished he had not brought up the subject. She did not want Marc to continue talking about her.

Regardless, Marc said, "We'll get to Kotzebue in time for Pat's wedding. But I, for one, am not looking forward to it."

Ara's heart sank. Obviously he was still in love with her.

"You've seen the way Curt follows her around every minute," Marc went on almost angrily. "He doesn't have the least idea that Pat needs room and lots of it. Curt wants to put her in some cage, where she will never, ever be happy."

Marc stepped closer to black wolf. "It's beyond me why Pat ever agreed to marry him."

Ara drew in her breath as Marc reached in through the bars, fearing at any moment the wolf might snap at him. But Marc seemed totally unafraid. He spoke calmly, soothingly, his movements slow and steady. "How's that leg today, boy?"

The huge animal's lip lifted in a warning snarl, but he didn't make a move. Neither did he cringe, but with proud indifference tolerated Marc's inspection of his paw.

"You're much better, pal," Marc said. "We will soon be able to make someone very happy—the day I can tell Pat I've set you free."

Ara's feeling of romance had fled. Overcome with disappointment, she wanted only to get back to the hotel. She started to walk toward the truck.

"Wait," Marc called. "You can't leave until you've seen my little gold-mining operation."

Ara hesitated, then turned back toward him.

Marc guided Ara around the cabin to a primitive wooden trough filled with running water. Beside it sat several buckets of sand from the beach. "Everyone out here pans for gold." He handed her an ancient gold-mining pan. "Try it out."

"What do I do?"

He dipped the pan into the water, scooping up sand. "You have to separate the sediment from the fine particles of gold."

Ara with a circular motion, shifted the contents.

"I'm not sure I'd recognize those particles if I saw them."

"Of course you will. Nothing looks like gold—but gold. See? You have a flake right there."

Ara laughed, her spirits once more lifting, as he placed her speck of gold into a small glass jar with the others he had sifted. "Your claim isn't exactly the Three Lucky Swedes," she observed, barely able to see the small dots of metal that clung to the sides of the glass.

"At this rate, it might take us the rest of our lives just to break even, but it's a start."

From then on, during the long drive back to Nome, they talked easily to one another again, about Alaska and Ara's future job, about the topics that concerned them most. "I hate to see careless trappers, like the one who caught the wolf," Ara said.

"I run across senseless slaughter more and more," Marc replied.

"I've always wondered why some people have no regard for wildlife, why they refuse to take care of our natural resources."

"They care about one thing only," Marc said, "bringing profit to themselves."

"And the rest of us pay for it."

Back at the hotel in Nome, as if to delay their parting, Marc suggested, "Let's take a little walk."

Ara drew the blue parka closer as they strolled along the shore in back of the hotel.

A thin, ragged man, spotting them from the street, left the sidewalk and cut across the sand toward them.

"I've got a real deal for you," he said confidentially to Marc. "A genuine gold nugget. You can buy it for the pretty lady." As he spoke, he drew out a tooth-size chunk of gold-colored rock suspended by a heavy chain.

Marc smiled. "How much will that cost me?"

"Because I must have money," he shot back importantly, "I'll make you a special bargain. It's like giving it to you." He held up the stone, dangling it in front of them, his eyes gleaming with anticipation. "What do you say to . . . fifteen dollars?"

Marc, eyes alight with amusement, looked at Ara. "For genuine gold, not a bad price."

"I wouldn't sell it," the man said anxiously, "if I didn't need the money."

"And I need the gold," Marc said, handing him a twenty. "You can keep the change."

Without even a thank-you or a glance back at them, the man pocketed the bill and scurried away. Marc said to Ara, "I just purchased for you a big chunk of worthless stone." He held it up. "But it is pretty, isn't it?"

Marc's blue eyes shone as he clasped the chain around her neck. "It's not real gold, of course. But then, isn't any object only worth the value you place upon it?"

Marc's fingers lingered, gently rearranging the dark strands of her hair, and Ara knew he meant the gift as a symbol of the pleasant day they had spent together.

"Anything that makes you smile at me like that," Marc said, "is more priceless than any gold nugget could ever be."

Chapter Ten

Marc had barely spoken since they had left the Nome airport. Ara cast a sideways glance at him. He seemed different today, as if her being seated beside him in the small plane was the last thing in the world that he wanted.

Although Ara wore the fake gold nugget Marc had given her last night, the magic of the gift had vanished. Ara thought of yesterday, the fun they had panning gold, seeing the new puppies. She wondered what accounted for the great change that had come over him, one that left her feeling sad and empty.

Marc finally spoke, his voice sounding muffled and far away over the grind of the small engine. "If you thought Nome was isolated, wait until you see Kotzebue."

"You had better tell me what to expect."

''The worst.''

She clung to the trace of a smile that had suddenly appeared and still lingered on his lips.

Ara forced her attention away from him, looking down at the uneven shoreline, jutting in and out, at times rising in rocky precipices.

''Look over there.'' Marc leaned forward, pointing toward the cliffs that lay below the wingtip.

Ara watched in fascination the gliding swoop of a large bird from the high rocks toward the sea.

''There are a lot of bald eagles here. They gather near the shore to feed on salmon.''

''Such magnificent birds.''

''Of course, the eagle is protected by federal law. But so much of our wildlife is endangered.'' He added, ''Some of the animals here, like the ribbon seal, follow the advance and retreat of ice on the Bering and Chukchi seas. Even though they're not easily available to hunters, that still doesn't protect them from exploitation.''

Soon they headed inland. The small plane roared steadily northeast across mountain peaks covered with snow, at other times falling away into flat, forested valleys spotted with lakes.

''Sometimes I dread landing,'' Marc said. ''Nothing ever goes wrong for me up here.''

''It would only have to once,'' Ara replied lightly as she gazed down into the vast depth of a shadowed valley.

Marc purposefully tilted the plane to give her a

wide, panoramic view of the untamed land that endlessly stretched to the east.

"This is Alaska," he said, "where dreams come
true."

The tiny craft leveled, then soared upward, as if it
had become one with the eagle she had a short time
ago watched. As they gained elevation, the thought
came to Ara that she would never be part of Marc's
dream. He had been describing himself instead of Pat
Neely yesterday when he had talked about the black
wolf that he intended someday to set free. In a round-
about way he was letting Ara know that he needed the
vast reaches of mountains and sky and wanted nothing, neither home nor family, to impede his flight or
his freedom.

Ara found herself for the first time feeling a closeness to her birth mother. Her mother couldn't have
helped knowing that Sam Neely, like Marc, belonged
to the outreaches of civilization, to some wild and jagged land such as Ara now viewed from the airplane
window.

The thought flashed in her mind like a brilliant light:
she must not allow herself to fall in love with Marc
Stewart. Even as the message came to her and she
caught his sun-cast image from the corner of her eye,
she wondered if the warning had come too late.

After a while Marc touched her arm. A great sweep
of sand, barren and brown against the blue of the water, thrust from the edges of the Seward Peninsula
back toward flat, rolling tundra.

"Some of those dunes are a hundred feet high," Marc said.

"The last thing I expected to see out here were sand dunes."

"They're caused by grinding glaciers." Marc paused. "You won't be expecting what you'll find in Kotzebue, either."

"What's it like?"

"A tiny village of Inupiat Eskimos. They live by fishing and hunting, mostly caribou. I'll be glad to be your guide while you're there."

"No doubt I'll need one."

"Kotzebue is the end of the line for the *Sea Rogue*. The ship will be docked there for three days, to load and unload cargo; then she'll head back south, the way we came. But I won't be going with them this trip," Marc added, his lips tightening. "Neither will Curt and Pat. They plan to stay and honeymoon in Kotzebue."

Ara, noting his resentment and lacking any reply, allowed her gaze to sweep over the photographs stuck haphazardly around the plane. Her eyes came to rest on a tiny, crumpled picture of Marc and Pat.

She drew in her breath. Marc had his arm around her, and Pat—Pat was wearing the blue parka that just yesterday Ara had worn. Without a doubt it was the same parka, one Pat must have left in his cabin, one Pat herself must have decorated, carefully stitching on those intricate, geometric designs.

Hurt rushed over Ara along with an awareness of just what was causing Marc's somber mood. Even though Marc didn't want to be tied down himself, the thought of Pat marrying someone else must cause him regret.

Ara, morosely silent, continued to watch the scenery, which instead of striking her as breathtakingly beautiful now looked barren and desolate.

She spotted Kotzebue as it first came into view, almost an island, the way the land jutted out into the sea. The sight of the tiny habitation perched on the very edge of nowhere took her by surprise.

The plane dipped precariously downward, steadied, came in level. Ara braced herself against the drag of the wheels on the small runway.

"I'll take you to the hotel; then we'll met later for dinner if you like."

"Thanks," Ara replied, attempting not to sound as bleak and remote as Kotzebue looked, "but I have some business I must see to."

Marc checked his watch. "It's still early, not quite ten. What if I meet you in the hotel lobby at three? That should give you plenty of time."

Wayfarer Charters in comparison to her father's office in Nome seemed ultramodern, sprawling and whitewashed. It sat at the far end of the small, flat strip of land that made up the boundaries of Kotzebue, the last in a line of shabby, weatherworn buildings.

In the water directly across the roadway two large, rusty ships, one of them precariously tilted, sat permanently docked. Retired ships, Ara thought, belonging to her father's business.

Inside the office, Curt, surrounded by papers, glanced up from his desk, fingers twining through his longish hair in a motion of exasperation. Ara couldn't help noticing that he looked very distraught and weary for a soon-to-be groom.

She drew forward and, without waiting for an invitation, sat down across from him. They looked at each other without speaking. His unhappiness made her identify with him, brought them close together. They had, after all, one thing in common—feeling pushed aside—and Pat Neely was the cause of it.

With no word about how or when she had arrived, Curt asked anxiously, "Have you seen Pat?"

Ara shook her head. "I've barely settled in."

"I was trying to discuss important matters with her a while ago, and she just got up and walked out." Once again lean fingers ran through his dark hair. "We've got lots of decisions to make. What to do with this mess." He shoved aside a stack of papers as he spoke. "She won't even talk to me about the business, which is sinking deeper and deeper into bankruptcy every day. But worse than that, she won't even discuss our marriage plans."

Curt looked across the desk at her imploringly. The white shirt and the rimless reading glasses made him seem more than ever the New York executive. Ara sympathized with his plight.

He certainly didn't deserve to be left alone to deal with the company's financial ruin, but there wasn't much Ara could do to help him. Neither did he deserve to be so totally committed to Pat, who he must surely realize was still in love with Marc.

"Pat's under a lot of pressure now."

"I know that. And I accepted the fact that she would not want to marry until after Sam was found and properly buried. It was Pat who came to me and said, 'Sam would want us to go ahead with our plans. Let's not wait.' Then, when I try to make wedding arrangements, what does she do? She just walks out."

"Give her some space. In time she'll be back wanting to talk to you."

"But why is she acting like this, Ara?"

Ara tried to lighten his despondent mood. "Haven't you heard? Woman are unpredictable."

She must have said the right thing. Curt pushed his chair away from the desk and leaned back, relaxing a little. "Here I'm talking to you about my own problems," he said, "when I should be dealing with yours."

"I didn't come here because of business. I just dropped by to see if you had any more news about Sam Neely."

"The Coast Guard is continuing to search for his body. As yet, they've found nothing." A determined edge crept into Curt's voice, as if he felt compelled to tell her what he himself did not want to face. "Sam's body may never be recovered. I saw his boat, at least what was left of it, when we docked at Nome. It's a sure thing, Ara; he didn't survive."

After a long, sad silence, Curt went on, "Whatever

business you had with Sam, you might just as well do
with me.''

Ara wanted to alleviate the pain that marked his
features. She felt a prompting to tell him she had seen
and talked with Sam Neely, one she cast aside by rising and ambling around the room. ''There's nothing
you can help me with.''

''Why not give it a try? I'll do my best.''

Before Ara could answer, the phone rang. The office
chair creaked as Curt pulled himself forward and lifted
the receiver. ''Wayfarer Charters.''

As Curt spoke in a quiet, businesslike manner, Ara
wandered over to the neat row of filing cabinets that
lined the back wall. In front of them sat an impressive
desk with a plaque lettered in gold, SAM NEELY. If only
she could search through his personal papers. They
might contain a clue that would shed some light on
the danger he was facing. At least she might find a
phone number or a note that would indicate where to
begin looking for him.

Curt's voice as he addressed the caller sharpened.
''He either wants to do business or he doesn't.''

An impatient pause followed.

''That's what you are hired to do. Don't expect me
to . . .'' Curt's hazel eyes settled on Ara and he made
an effort to restore polite formality. ''On the other
hand, it might be a good idea that you called me. How
much cargo are we talking about?''

Ara, not wanting to interfere with his conversation,
strolled over to the window and stood looking out at
the ancient boats. Through the misty ocean light she

could make out the name of the one nearest her, *Arctic Belle*. The ship's "belle" days were long over, her mast fallen, the boards on her side rotting and warped.

Behind her Curt, still on the phone, had fallen into a sullen silence. Ara's gaze dropped to the iron window lock. Curt wouldn't notice if she reached over and turned the latch. Then, later, after he had left for the night, she could come back and go through her father's papers.

Ara leaned closer to the window, her body hiding the quick motion of her hand as she undid the lock.

"Of course the *Sea Rogue* will sail on Thursday as scheduled," Curt said irritably.

He listened, frowning, during another long pause.

"I see we're not going to resolve anything over the phone. Let's just meet and discuss this in person. No, it would be better if I came to you. Let's say fifteen minutes."

Curt brusquely replaced the receiver. "Sam's absence has caused so many problems. I'm going to have to lock up for a while."

After the harsh tone he had just used to the caller, Ara was surprised by his sudden change, now boyishly charming. "We'll all be staying at the same hotel. No choice here. Only one. So do me a favor, will you, Ara? Try to find out for me what's wrong with Pat."

Intending to make good her promise to Curt and have a heart to-heart talk with Pat, Ara went to the hotel. When she reached Pat's room, Ara tapped on the door.

She waited, both anticipating and dreading the meeting.

The minute she answered the door, Ara was aware of how different Pat looked from the morning they had parted in Nome. Ara had not thought Pat's exuberance would ever totally abandon her, or that those warm blue eyes could ever frost over and become so unapproachable.

Ara waited in awkward silence for some friendly greeting or for an invitation to enter. Receiving neither, she said, "I'd like to talk to you, but if this isn't a good time . . ."

Pat let go of the door she was holding and stepped back into the room. Ara noted the slump to her shoulders as she crossed to the window and sank despondently into one of the overstuffed chairs that faced the sea.

Pat's eyes were red-rimmed, and Ara knew she had been crying. Her heart sank. Had she received some troubling news about Sam Neely? Or was she grieving because he was missing at this important time in her life?

"Pat, what's wrong?"

Pat waved her hand in a despairing gesture, as if she would like to brush the whole world away.

Ara took a step or two closer. She was gripped by concern, enough, even, to be tempted to tell Pat that she had seen and talked to Sam Neely, that he was safe, at least for now.

Ara's father had found a way to contact her. She had believed that he had contacted Pat, too, which accounted for her decision to go on with her wedding. Now she wondered, as she stared at Pat, if that were true. If it wasn't, it could mean only one thing: that Sam Neely didn't trust her.

"I know this is a hard time for you," Ara said, "not knowing what happened to your uncle."

For a very long time Pat remained silent, dabbing at her eyes with a tissue, the way she might do at a funeral service.

"There's even more to it than that," she said finally. "I find I'm having second thoughts about getting married."

"Why don't you just postpone the wedding? Curt will understand."

"I'll feel the same way then, whenever it is, as I do now." Pat paused, then went on in a strange, hollow way. "Ara, have you ever been in love?"

Clearly Pat wasn't thinking of Curt. An image of Marc's face appeared to Ara as she answered. "I know what it must be like."

"Did you ever think you knew someone . . . and then found out that you didn't know them at all?"

"What are you saying, Pat? That you aren't in love with Curtis?"

Pat turned away. "I'm saying I don't think there's going to be any wedding."

Ara, unable to convince Pat to join her for lunch, went alone to the hotel dining room. Farley Riggs, suave and elegant, sat by the window, the sea framed behind him. He was just finishing his meal. Hal Bruins, idle, as usual, occupied the chair across from him.

The captain, not appearing to be the least bit surprised at seeing her, rose as Ara approached. ''You didn't stay in Nome long.''

''Long enough.''

''I don't think you're going to like Kotzebue any better.''

With those words Farley Riggs politely excused himself and left, but Hal Bruins remained. Ara found his smile particularly offensive.

''Have a chair, mate.''

Ara sat across from him and ordered a roast beef sandwich and a cup of coffee.

His impudent gaze, never leaving her, made Ara uneasy. She tried to make small talk with him, but he remained boorishly unresponsive. Not until her sandwich arrived did he speak, and then his words sounded clipped and rude. ''Why are you here?''

''To attend Curt and Pat's wedding.''

''There isn't going to be a wedding. I'd bet my passport on that.''

What did they all know that Ara didn't? ''Why do you think Pat has had a change of heart?'' Ara paused, then speculated, ''I suppose she has decided, after all, to wait until her uncle is found.''

''That might take a lifetime, mate. Anyway, Sam wouldn't want to be found. He wouldn't relish being buried in some icy little grave plot. He liked the sea. Pat knows that as well as anyone else. She would go ahead with the wedding, all right, if Marc Stewart would quit interfering.''

Ara felt a tug at her heart. Trying to avoid Hal Bruins's bold stare, she looked away from him out the window, asking, ''Why would Marc want to stop her from marrying Curt?''

''Simple math, babe.'' He leaned closer. ''Pat now has full authority to continue running Sam's business. In other words, with the old man dead or out of the picture, as long as he doesn't show up, Pat has total control of the company, lock, stock, and barrel.'' Ara could see Hal Bruins's face reflected in the glass. His slack, wet lips and pale eyes looked singularly evil.

Ara faced him again, saying steadily, ''Marc said he was engaged to her once, but it didn't work out for them.''

''That's because Marc,'' Hal said slowly, ''threw her over. But things have changed. Now that Uncle's gone, Pat's become a hell of a lot more attractive.''

Hal's smile widened. ''Marc Stewart knows a good thing when he sees it. He's doing everything he can to cut Curt out and marry himself a million-dollar operation.''

''But Sam Neely's business is on the verge of bankruptcy.''

''Now just who told you that?'' Hal Bruins asked insolently. ''Wayfarer Charters has never been in such good shape. The company's making money hand over fist.''

Chapter Eleven

In spite of the clouds of doubt she felt hanging over Marc, Ara found herself conscientiously checking her watch, anxiously awaiting three o'clock, the time Marc would be meeting her in the hotel lobby. Anticipation, the kind she had never experienced in her years of casual dating, gripped her. She showered and took time selecting the perfect outfit, black slacks that fit just right and a red silk blouse that she knew complemented her dark hair.

Despite the lengthy preparations, Ara was totally unprepared for seeing Marc the very moment she stepped out into the corridor. He stood at the end of the long hallway, deep in some private conversation with Pat. Neither of them noticed her as she stopped, feeling stunned by the way Marc stepped closer to Pat, as if he were about to enfold her in his arms.

116

Ara, her excitement over their afternoon together dashed, not wanting to be seen, crossed quickly to the stairway. She hurried down into the lobby, vacant except for a maid who solemnly straightened magazines on a coffee table. The maid spoke to her, then shuffled on, leaving Ara alone.

Hal Bruins's words rang into the emptiness. "Marc threw her over. . . . He's doing everything he can to cut Curt out and marry himself a million-dollar operation."

Even though she didn't want to see him, part of her listened intently for his step. When he at last came down into the lobby, he drew to a stop at the foot of the stairs. Unlike when he was talking to Pat, he maintained the wide space that separated them.

Without his usual smile, Marc looked older, harder. But this didn't distract from his handsomeness. That sober image of him, the burning intensity of his eyes, caused a strange catch in her breath.

"Something's come up, Ara. I'm not going to be free this afternoon."

At first Ara was too stunned to reply; then she said, as if Marc's rejection had not hurt her, "That's all right. There's some things I ought to be doing myself."

Marc's frown deepened. "I don't want you to leave the hotel, Ara. Not under any circumstance."

Ara made no reply.

"There's a lot happening here that you don't know about, Ara." His next words sounded less like an appeal, more like a threat. ''What you don't know might be the difference between life and death.''

He reached the front exit, then turned back again, his eyes boring into hers. ''Why don't you go up and talk to Pat? She could use the company. I'll contact you as soon as I can.''

Since Marc had canceled their meeting, there was no longer any need to delay searching for her father. Ara crossed to a side exit that opened onto a patio enclosed by a wooden fence.

Farley Riggs, elbows resting on the railing, seemed aware of her presence without ever looking around. ''There's no place on earth quite like Kotzebue.''

As he spoke in his quiet, calm way, he did not take his eyes from the sea, from the nearby dock where shouts drifted to them. ''See those men? Inupiat fishermen.''

Ara drew forward to stand beside him. The small group was preparing to set off in a kayak. They wore white parkas, sealskin pants, and waterproof mukluks to protect them from the chill waters.

''A walrus was caught today, and fellow hunters are calling for extra hands,'' the captain said.

''Eskimos are the only ones who can hunt walrus, aren't they?''

Farley Riggs answered in his slow, thoughtful way, ''Only for food or for use in the native craft of carving ivory.''

''I saw some beautiful carvings when we were in Lone Port.''

"Ivory carving is an important part of the native economy."

"Then you must transport a lot of it."

The captain answered, "We don't transport any ivory. It's illegal to export uncarved tusks."

Farley Riggs watched the fishermen a while longer; then, as if by a summons, he straightened up and turned to her with a long, appraising look. "You are beginning to puzzle me," he said. "I would really like to know what connection you have with Sam Neely."

"He is . . . a friend of the family."

"I find it hard to believe that Sam would give you, some acquaintance, a pass to board the dilapidated old *Sea Rogue*." He continued to gaze at her, his dark eyes steady. "I can't understand why you got off at Nome, then out of the blue show up in Kotzebue."

"As I told you before, Sam was going to meet me on the freighter. I didn't know exactly what to do when he didn't."

"Was this meeting of that much importance?" Farley Riggs studied her. Seeming to determine that Ara was not going to confide in him, he said, "If I had a brother, I would want him to be Sam Neely. There's nothing I wouldn't do for him, or, if it's comes to that, for his memory. This might be a good thing for you to remember . . . if you should ever need a friend."

Leaving Captain Riggs, Ara wandered past square-shaped houses, modern-day igloos built of wood rather than ice and snow, many of them topped with caribou antlers. The village was so small she could circle it in

its entirety without much effort—a cluttering of hous-
ing, a general store—a tiny settlement embraced by
the arms of the sea. A flat, desolate tundra stretched
behind it, heightening the impression of a lonely out-
post on some cold, lost fringe of civilization.

In the glow of midsummer Kotzebue looked pleasant, even charming. But Ara imagined that in the long,
dark winter months it would be a desolate place, even
more cut off from the mainstream than Lone Port, the
world beyond the tiny settlement a wasteland of ice,
howling winds and blinding white snow.

She made inquiries concerning her father, talking to
the clerk at the store, a man working on an old truck
outside his house. Everyone she asked knew Sam
Neely, each seemed troubled over the report that his
boat was found but that he was missing. But it was,
after all, news they had heard before concerning other
sailors, fathers, sons, brothers, who had set out to sea,
never to return.

As the afternoon wore on, a light rain began, driz-
zling through grim clouds of fog. Ara checked her
watch—after six. Wayfarer Charters would now be
closed for the day.

She waited in front of her father's office to make
sure no one was around; then she found an old crate
out back and used it for a step up to the high window.
Effortlessly she slipped inside.

The large room had a dim, dreary cast to it. She
was going to need the flashlight she had brought along.
Ara opened the filing cabinet nearest her, bypassed

sections marked *Transfers, Docking Fees, Repairs,* and took out folders filed under *Shipping Orders.*

From the consistent dates on the sheets she examined, Ara could see that Wayfarer Charters had an abundance of regular cargo runs. But without a complete audit there wasn't any way for her to determine profit and loss.

In another cabinet Ara found files labeled *Charter Runs.* All of them concerned ships—Marc must keep his own records on the air flights. But what was she really going to tell by these transactions? She finally realized she could study every ledger in the office and still know no more about the state of her father's business than she did right now.

If Sam Neely were here in Kotzebue, someone, perhaps a friend, must know of his whereabouts. She would try to find a note, a phone number, an address among the personal items in his desk.

Ara had started to cross the room when she saw through the front window a form emerging from thick white layers of fog. She clicked off the flashlight and shrank back against the filing cabinet where she had just replaced the folders.

The form, a man wearing a dark, hooded raincoat, stopped just outside the building. He appeared to be looking around for someone. Then he turned toward the door, and she could make out his features—Marc.

Ara held her breath as Marc stopped. She could see his face clearly, the spray of rain glowing across golden hair. He turned back and gazed around again.

Could he be looking for her, or had he planned to meet with someone at this office tonight?

She knew, even without proof, that illegal operations were being carried on by Wayfarer Charters. Marc might very well be playing some part in this scheme.

Ara watched alertly, not daring to make any movement. Suddenly, with a decisive step, Marc headed for the door.

Ara's heart pounded. She couldn't allow him to find her here. Her glance fell to the window, but she knew she would never be able to get through it before he entered the room. Taking a great risk, with catlike speed she darted toward her father's huge desk. She ducked behind it and waited.

A rattle sounded as Marc tried the door. She listened tensely. Would he be taking out a key? She heard no other sound.

For a long time she dared not make any move, but when nothing further happened, she cast a quick glance toward the door. She could no longer see the dark outline of Marc's raincoat. Ara took a steadying breath and forced herself to remain where she was for a while longer. Then she crossed to the window and looked out into the empty fog.

Assured that Marc had left, she finally returned to her father's desk and began opening drawers. The top one contained paper clips, pens, tape—no address book or scribbled notations.

In the top drawer on the right-hand side, she found a mountain of personal correspondence. Anxiously she shuffled through the letters. She found a birthday card from Pat to "a special uncle," beneath it, a letter that hadn't been opened. She quickly broke the seal. It was only a dinner party invitation from Anchorage, one delivered after Sam had turned up missing. She placed it at the bottom of the stack, then abruptly stopped— a letter from Silver Lake, Montana.

Ara opened it with nervous fingers. It was from Glenda Carr, a nurse at the hospital. Ara remembered her well, a kind, dutiful woman who had stayed by her mother's side continuously during her last illness.

Ara skimmed the short message. "Betty Londell, a patient of mine and a dear friend, wanted me to write to you, but she slipped into a coma before she could dictate the letter. I keep worrying about this. It seems as if I failed her, as if I hadn't carried out her final wish, one that was of utmost importance to her. She had discussed with me the message she wanted you to receive. It was very brief: 'Please forgive me for never letting you know you had a daughter.' "

Since her father had told her he didn't want anyone to know who she was, he wouldn't have left this letter in his desk. Ara clicked on the flashlight and read the date on the postmark. Evidently Sam Neely had not received Glenda Carr's message. It was postmarked the same day as the invitation from Anchorage.

Then why was it open?

Had some secretary merely glanced at it and placed it in the drawer with her father's other correspondence? Or did this mean that one of them—or all of them at Wayfarer Charters—knew exactly who Ara was?

Just in case it hadn't already been found and read, Ara took the letter with her.

She walked back toward town along the docks, past where the *Sea Rogue* set anchored. A coldness from the water's depth oozed up through the heavy mist, causing Ara to draw her rain jacket tightly around her.

In bright sunlight the little village had looked forsaken enough, but its dreariness, its seclusion, became magnified by the heavy clouds and the rain. She could barely make out the square, bulky outline of the hotel.

As she drew closer, she saw that Hal Bruins stood outside talking to a teenager, who Ara thought, although she couldn't see him clearly, must be of Eskimo descent.

The conversation between the two possessed no signs of casual friendliness. In fact, what passed between them seemed totally business-oriented, a matter of vital importance. The minute the boy left, so did Hal Bruins, hurrying off in the opposite direction. Whatever news Hal Bruins had been given, he clearly had not liked.

Instead of going into the hotel, Ara followed after Hal. He walked in the center of the road, taking long, quick strides, his eyes straight ahead. Ara kept a wide distance between them.

At the crossroads, Hal turned left. Ara, thinking he might be aware of her behind him, that he might be lying in wait, hidden behind the row of buildings, slowed her steps.

Ara was relieved to find Hal far ahead as she rounded the turn. She was going to have to walk briskly so she wouldn't lose him in the obscurity of fog.

At the end of the row of houses, Hal left the street, cutting into a cluttered yard, where he was lost to her view. Again Ara stopped, wondering how she was going to get close enough to know what was going on and at the same time keep Hal from seeing her.

Where Hal had approached the house from the front, Ara crept around to the side.

Hal must have stormed in without being admitted, for he had left the door wide open. She couldn't see who he was talking to, but she could hear Hal's loud voice, almost shouting, "A deal is a deal. And we had one. A done one. You can't go raising prices, demanding more money, not right in the middle of a contract!"

The voice that answered was very low. Ara had trouble making out his words, words that, like Hal's, possessed a clipped accent. "I don't like . . . this dealing with you anymore. It's going to get me into trouble."

Hal Bruins spoke angrily. "No one even knows about you. We're the ones who take all the risk!"

"What about Farley Riggs? I don't like the way he's been looking at me. I think he knows."

"You're letting yourself get all worked up over

nothing," Hal replied. "The captain has no idea what's going on."

"I want more for this load," the other man said abruptly. "Take it or leave it. And this time I want the money, all of it, before I deliver the goods."

"We've always worked things out before. What's got into you?"

The voice of the man Hal addressed remained at the same calm level. "I don't like some of the things I've been hearing."

"Not you, Willard, it's the boss who's not going to like what he'll be hearing. I'll tell you right now, he's not going to put up with it. He's not going to pay you a cent more."

"Then go buy from someone else."

"You want to play hardball, do you?" Hal asked threateningly.

"Don't try to push me around, Mr. Bruins. It's just not going to work."

"I'll talk to him. That's all I can do."

"No," the other man corrected Hal, "I want to talk to him."

"He won't agree to that."

"Then tell him the deal is off."

It took some time for Hal to bridge the cold space of silence. "OK. I'll arrange to have you meet with him. How about tonight? Be at the Wayfarer Charter office the minute it gets dark."

Chapter Twelve

After the conversation Ara had overheard between Hal Bruins and the unseen Willard, she could believe Farley Riggs was a friend instead of an enemy. Her first impulse was to find the *Sea Rogue*'s captain and tell him exactly what she had found out.

Ara knocked on the door to his room, but no one answered; then she began looking around the hotel. Her search led her to the patio where earlier today they had talked. She stopped at French doors, half expecting to find Farley Riggs seated in one of the chairs that lined the wall outside.

Instead she found Pat and Curt standing by the fence. Ara started toward them, but Curt's raised voice caused her to pause and step back a little. It was obvious that the soon-to-be newlyweds were in the midst of an argument.

127

''What's the matter with you, Pat? Why won't you talk to me? What have I done to make you so angry?''

''I'm not angry,'' Pat replied, keeping her face turned away from him.

''Is this about Sam?'' Curt asked gently. He attempted to take Pat's arm, but she pulled away.

''It's about . . . a lot of things.''

A note of suspicion crept into Curt's tone. ''What was Marc doing here this afternoon? Why do you have to see him all the time? What were you two talking about?''

''This has nothing to do with Marc,'' Pat replied shortly.

Pat's quavering voice, strained, unconvincing, made Ara's heart plunge.

''Pat, don't let Marc come between us. You know what he's like.''

Pat made no reply.

Curt made a gallant attempt to restore his usual mildness. ''Honey, all you have is the wedding-day jitters,'' he said placatingly. ''I've got them, too,'' he added, attempting once more to put his arm around her.

What the two lovers didn't need right now was interruption. Ara slipped quietly back through the doorway. Curt's voice, now controlled and confident, drifted after her. ''Once we're married everything's going to be all right. You just wait and see.''

The town was quiet except for the occasional barking of a dog as Ara set out alone to the office of Wayfarer

Charters. She followed the dirt road along the sea, glancing, but not stopping, as she passed the *Sea Rogue*, which loomed formidable and ghostly through the thick layer of fog.

Just ahead the sprawling, modern building that housed Wayfarer Charters blended with the ethereal white of mist. Across from it, bobbing in the deep water, was the vague outline of the derelict ship, *Arctic Belle*.

Ara wasn't sure when, if ever, darkness would truly fall, but the sky filled with gusts of murky clouds would provide adequate cover. She had plenty of time to find a place to conceal herself so she could wait and see who showed up for the clandestine meeting Hal Bruins had set up this afternoon.

She sincerely wished Farley Riggs were beside her now. She would be calmed by his capable, self-assured manner. She had been suspicious of him before, but now believed the crates he had ordered unloaded at Lone Port were in fact not contraband—which certainly didn't mean the *Sea Rogue* was free of smugglers and thieves. Tonight would be a different story, and Ara was going to know exactly who was behind all these illegal dealings.

She had only to hide herself, to wait and find out who the boss was who would meet with Hal Bruins and Willard.

Visibility improved at closer range. Here in Kotzebue there must be no need for night watchmen and security guards. The office was totally vacant, just as it had been when she had entered it to go through her father's papers.

She must find a place where she could watch the entrance of the Wayfarer office without being seen. Her gaze fell at once on the *Arctic Belle*. Ara crossed the dirt road and headed toward the big, creaking hulk of a ship, permanently docked. A NO TRESPASSING sign hung from a chain across the wooden plank that connected the boat with the dock.

She slipped under it and made her way carefully across the dangerously sloping deck. The *Arctic Belle*, much smaller than the *Sea Rogue*, had only one cabin. She pushed open a rusted metal door, which led into a large room. The front of it was a steerage area. The wheel remained intact, but the dials that flanked it were broken or missing, making it look like the dashboard of some long abandoned, junkyard car.

The front was faced with windows, caked with dirt and salt, in places shattered. Ara had found the perfect vantage point. Through these obscure, splintered windows, she could view the Wayfarer Charters office, and no one would ever see her or suspect that anyone would be aboard the ancient *Arctic Belle*.

Ara checked her watch—much too early for the appointed meeting. Waiting was going to be difficult. She glanced uneasily around the disheveled arrangement of furniture that no one had bothered to salvage. Several tall cabinets, tilting on the uneven floor, had been pushed out into the center of the room. In the eerie semidarkness she imagined Hal Bruins or some other thief hiding behind them, watching her every move.

She struggled to drive out the frightening image.

The interior of the abandoned ship's cabin bore a tomblike coldness. That and the sound of splashing waves caused Ara to shiver and draw her jacket closer around her.

Not quite able to judge how much time had elapsed, Ara kept to her post, her gaze seldom straying from the office doorway. Suddenly every muscle stiffened. Every sense became more alert. A lone figure in a dark coat was cutting through the mist in front of Wayfarer Charters.

Ara saw through the haze of gray fog a flash of golden hair. She drew in her breath and flattened herself against the wall, even though there was no way he would see her.

Tears stung Ara's eyes, made a lump in her throat. Marc Stewart, Marc, the boss that Hal Bruins and Willard would meet here tonight.

That was the reason Marc hadn't wanted her to fly with him to Kotzebue. He was afraid her search for her father would in some way interfere with his shady deal.

Feeling crushed and betrayed by the knowledge that Marc was a common thief, a smuggler, Ara watched him vanish around the north corner of the building.

One part of Ara jumped to Marc's defense. If he were guilty, he would simply go inside the office and wait for Hal and Willard so they could negotiate their illegal transaction. Another part of her insisted that

Marc preferred waiting outside, so he could appear or not appear, in any event, so he could gain some advantage.

A long time passed. She did not see any movement at all from outside the murky panes of glass.

In the tense stillness, broken only by rising waves, a distinct noise came to her. Metal clanged against metal, as if someone had removed the chain that dangled in front of the boarding plank.

She couldn't stay in this cabin. If someone should enter back here by the windows she would be trapped. She quickly crossed to the door opposite the one she had entered.

Once she was out on the deck, a swirling gale tousled her hair, tugged at her jacket. Maybe it had just been a blast of wind that had caused the sound she had heard. But even as that thought came to her, she knew better. She was certain she was no longer alone on the *Arctic Belle*.

The floorboards, tilted precariously to the right, made walking difficult. Ara kept remembering how very deep the water around the *Arctic Belle* had looked. The encroaching sounds of the icy sea kept her close to the cabin wall.

Ara made her slow, cautious way toward the back of the boat. Once there she would be able to see the other side of the deck and with any luck get a glimpse of the person who had boarded.

A rapid clack of footsteps sounded from behind her. Ara caught a gleam of silver as a strong hand snaked around her neck. She winced as the heavy metal of a watchband crushed against her throat, shutting off her breath. Ara, unable to move her head, unable to see her assailant, fought back with the strength of panic.

A fierce blow struck her right temple, jolting her, causing a searing pain that spread like an all-engulfing fire. Blackness blotted her vision. She would have slumped to the floor were it not for the talonlike hands that clutched her arms, that wrenched them behind her.

Stunned, fighting against unconsciousness, Ara could not stop the force that propelled her toward the back of the boat. A violent shove sent her crashing against the railing, whose rotten supports gave way and sent her hurling over the side.

The shock of icy water stopped her plummet into unconsciousness. In a desperate effort to save herself, Ara's fingers grazed the side of the boat, finding nothing at all to hang on to.

It wasn't far to the wooden dock, to solid ground. She tried to swim, but waves tossed her back toward the boat.

She could feel a torturous, penetrating coldness. She was fast losing strength, struggling now just to stay afloat.

Ara was growing steadily weaker, floundering. In a frenzy of fear she realized she was not going to be able to save herself. She was going to die.

Maybe it wouldn't be that bad, sinking, sinking into the icy embrace of the sea. She looked up for one last time, the darkness of the ocean blending with the blackness that blotched her vision.

A face peered down at her from the deck of the *Arctic Belle*—a rough, familiar face with curling hair and a dark, grizzled beard—her father's face.

Chapter Thirteen

Very gradually Ara became aware of the sound of an idling motor. At first it seemed far in the distance, but it grew louder until it encircled her. It soon dawned upon her that she was lying flat on her back under a covering of canvas. The cold boards beneath her rose and fell uncertainly, as if they were being buffeted by angry waves.

Where was she? How had she gotten from the sea into a boat? What had happened to her father?

With great effort Ara opened her eyes. The small craft was adrift far from shore. Marc was leaning over her. In the misty darkness his features were indistinct, but she caught the gleam of moisture that clung to his hair and clothing.

''Are you all right, Ara?'' His words were almost overpowered by the drone of the motor. He removed the cloth he had been holding to her temple. ''I don't think you were struck hard enough to cause anything more than swelling and discomfort.''

Intent on making sure, he examined her eyes, flashing the beam from the flashlight into one, then the other. ''If you think you need to see a doctor . . .''

Ara brushed this suggestion aside. Through lips cold and numb, Ara gasped, ''I saw him. He was looking down at me.''

Marc placed a restraining hand against her shoulder as she tried to rise. ''Lie still, Ara.''

''Why would he . . . ?''

The only answer that came formed in her own thoughts—he wanted her dead so he could inherit what had just been passed to her, the Londell money. But Sam Neely was her father—how could that be? How could he without a qualm strike out at her and watch her flounder and drown in the freezing Arctic water?

The protective numbness of a moment ago was beginning to fade, leaving fingers of ice that made her entire body tremble. ''Where are we? Where are we going?''

''Somewhere safe. I'll explain everything to you later. For now, just don't try to talk.''

Marc turned to a long, metal box attached to the boat's side. He shuffled through raincoats and tools and found jeans and a sweatshirt. ''You must get out of those wet clothes. Can you manage that?''

''I think so.''

''The trip to the cabin usually takes about twenty

minutes. But I'll get there as fast as I can.'' Marc stood up and, swaying a little from a jolting wave, started back to the wheel.

Ara removed the soaking blouse. She had worn it just for him. She tossed it aside, slipping quickly into the heavy shirt, then pulling on the jeans. The effort left her exhausted. She remained huddled beneath the heavy canvas.

Bombarded by the noise of wind and water, Ara gazed upward at the dark sky. Her father, the boss Hal was taking the man Willard to meet, must have boarded the *Arctic Belle* for the same reason she had, to conceal himself. But her father would have no reason to hide from his fellow conspirators. Unless, instead of negotiating with Willard, Sam Neely's plans were to murder him, to rid himself of a rebellious witness who he no longer considered of any use to him.

The thought sickened her. She closed her eyes and tried not to think at all. After a while she began to feel the heat from the dry clothes, from the heavy cover, begin to penetrate her limbs. With the warmth came a sense of safety. Her thoughts drifted back to Silver Lake, Montana. She was lying peacefully in her bedroom, listening to Mom and Dad in the kitchen, discussing the day's events over early morning coffee. Melvin Londell, kind and good, he was her *real* father. She clung to the thought of home and found the terror she felt beginning to slip away.

In the small bedroom of the cabin Marc took her to, Ara had exchanged the boat floor for a comfortable bed, the canvas for a thick down comforter. Marc had brought her stew and hot chocolate, which she had just finished.

He came back into the room and set a glass on the stand beside her bed. ''Medication,'' he said. ''After you drink this and get a good night's sleep, you'll be as good as new.''

Marc did not leave the room at once, but stood gazing down at her. He was so handsome—Ara's rescuer, her hero.

''Thanks for saving my life.''

Marc gave her a small, gentle smile.

He must have been suspicious of her father all along. That was why he hadn't wanted her to go along with him on this dangerous search for Sam Neely. She wondered if he had enough proof of her father's guilt to take to the police.

The thought of her father's guilt made her feel sick and weary. She certainly didn't feel up to discussing tomorrow or what would happen to her father once they turned him in.

''How did you know where to find me?''

''Let's say I was looking for you. But let's not talk now.'' Marc handed her the glass filled with milky liquid. ''You need to relax, to sleep.''

With those words, Marc leaned close to her, his warm lips ever so briefly meeting hers; then abruptly he left the room.

Ara felt drained and groggy already. She did not need her thoughts to be further clouded by heavy medication. Not wanting Marc to know she hadn't taken the sedative he offered, she poured the liquid into what was left of the hot chocolate, then set the empty glass back on the stand.

The door Marc had passed through remained slightly ajar. Light from the adjoining room sent a soft glow into the semidarkness. She listened to the crackling of the fire, to Marc's footsteps. After a long time her troubled thoughts began to drift and she slept.

Ara awoke with a start. The muffled conversation from the next room had a sinister ring to it. She listened alertly and was able to make out the words.

''I waited for a long time for Hal or Buddy to show up.'' The deep, gruff voice could belong to no one but Sam Neely. ''I don't know why they didn't. All I can figure is that they spotted either you or Ara and that scared them off.''

''I wouldn't be too concerned about it,'' Marc replied. ''I think we can count on their going ahead with the load with or without any special arrangements.''

A long, heavy silence fell. ''Why didn't you take her to Anchorage like I told you to?''

Marc answered, ''I had no choice. You have no idea how stubborn she is. She would have gotten on the next plane. She was determined to come out here, with or without me.''

Ara, heart pounding, propped herself up in bed. She had been dead wrong. Marc and her father were co-conspirators, partners in crime. A sense of horror stole over her as her father continued speaking.

''She knows way too much now. If only you had

done what I said from the beginning, kept her completely away from Wayfarer Charters.''

''It's a little too late to think about that,'' Marc broke in grimly. ''The question is: what are we going to do with her now? If we turn her loose, she'll go right to the police. She'll ruin everything.''

A long, tense silence followed before Sam Neely spoke again. ''We can't let her get back on the *Sea Rogue*, that's for sure. There's just too much at stake.''

A cold chill gripped Ara. She was grateful she could not see her father's face, which she knew would be cold and hard, the way it had been when he had stared down at her as she had floundered in the icy water. She was relieved that she couldn't see his wrist, and the silver watchband that had brutally cut into her throat, choking off her breath.

''I've given her a strong sedative,'' Marc told him. ''She'll be out like a light for the rest of the night. And by ten o'clock tomorrow morning the *Sea Rogue* will have sailed.''

Sam Neely's tone sounded menacing. ''After it's all over, we'll have all the time in the world to deal with this willful daughter of mine.''

Marc must have no idea, even though the two of them were working together, that her father would have reason to want her dead. He must not know that Sam Neely himself had purposely tried to kill her tonight.

Marc had saved her life, pulled her from the water, but that did not make him innocent. He had taken her out to this forsaken cabin to prevent her from interfering with their plans.

Without doubt Marc Stewart was one of her father's henchmen. He had brought her here, making her think he was her rescuer—when, in fact, she was his prisoner. She had been kidnapped.

Chapter Fourteen

The voices from the next room steadily lost volume, as if Marc and her father were walking away from her. The front door opened and closed, and soon Ara heard the sound of an engine starting. The vehicle drove off, leaving in its wake a total silence.

All Ara had seen when she had entered the cabin with Marc had been a jagged shoreline behind which stretched an endless tundra with nothing, not even trees, visible on the horizon. But at least there was a road leading away from here, one that must connect with someplace—if not Kotzebue, then another small village.

Ara slipped out of bed and watched through the crack of open door. She had hoped that both of them had left, but Marc was coming back inside the cabin. To her dismay he continued walking in her direction.

She lost no time getting back into bed and snuggling her face down against the pillow, eyes closed.

As Marc looked in on her, Ara tried to keep her breathing slow and regular. He did not stay long, just a moment, then returned to the next room.

Now was the time to make her escape. She must act quickly and noiselessly. In the closet she found some boots and a jacket, which she hurriedly slipped on over the jeans and sweatshirt Marc had given her on the boat. As she crossed to the window, she glimpsed Marc, her captor, seated beside the door, where, no doubt, he planned to stay, keeping vigilant guard over her as she slept.

It wouldn't be long until Marc would check on her again. By the time he missed her, she must be safely out of sight. And that, according to the flat landscape, would be a tall order.

Careful not to make any noise, holding her breath, Ara slowly pushed open the window. Feeling clumsy in the ill-fitting clothes and in the boots many sizes too large for her, Ara managed to ease herself through the small opening and climb down to the ground.

Her first impulse was to head toward the boat that had brought them here. But she had seen Marc remove the keys, and she knew she would never be able to get it started without them. Besides, it was much too close to the cabin.

Ara, fighting against a strong prompting to run, forced herself to walk, quickly, steadily. She followed the tracks left by her father's vehicle.

She did not dare to look back until she had put some

distance between her and the cabin. When she did stop and glance around, the small dwelling looked isolated and solitary, a swaybacked shack sitting all alone near the sea. The only sign of occupation was the fire that sent smudges of black from the chimney into the obscurely white sky.

Nothing else save the curling smoke stirred.

Marc, thinking she was sedated and fast asleep, was not likely to miss her for a long time. If only she knew what to do, what direction to head. The grass was higher here so that she could no longer locate the imprint of the wheels made by her father's vehicle.

What if she was to encounter nothing out here in this remote wilderness, no one, not even an Eskimo fisherman?

Casting her fears aside, Ara increased her pace. As her steps hit spongy grass of the tundra, she could feel a quiver as the earth sank beneath her feet. From time to time she would swipe at the swarms of mosquitoes, but she did not allow the annoying, buzzing insects to slow her gait.

What would she do if Sam Neely, returning from whatever errand had sent him from the cabin, were to spot her? She saw again the vivid image of his face peering down into the water at her. The thought made her shiver, caused her legs to feel weak. She might have been better off staying with Marc. Marc, after all, had saved her once. She should have taken the chance that he would not let Sam Neely harm her.

Ara, overcome by a sudden exhaustion, forced herself to keep walking. The chill, damp air made her head throb. Breathing became more and more difficult.

Midway through the level of tundra, she had to stop and catch her breath. Overhead the clouds were beginning to thin and clear, making visibility sharp. In the far, far distance the flatland ended, halted by jagged mountain peaks, sharp-etched against the sky. Nowhere in between did she note any indication of human habitation.

Ara could see that the slender projection of land where she now stood jutted far out into the sea, just as it did in Kotzebue. She noticed as she continued to cut across it that the shoreline she was approaching was ribbed with rocks, scrub, and trees. It was wise to stay close to this line of cover, Ara thought, just in case she needed a place to hide.

She had no sooner thought this than she caught the faint sound of a motor coming from the direction of the cabin. Sam Neely had returned. Marc and her father must have discovered that she was gone. That meant they were setting out to look for her.

Ara began running toward the cover of rocks and brush. Her footsteps slipped on the marshy ground and sent her hurling forward. Ignoring the pain where her knee had struck a loose rock, she struggled to her feet again and darted down a stony slope that fell off sharply toward the sea.

She flattened herself against rock and earth and waited.

The sound of the engine grew louder. The vehicle

must have stopped very close to where she lay concealed.

The engine clicked off, leaving a silence broken only by the swarm of insects.

Soon she heard the harsh slam of a door, which was followed by Marc's words: "She has a head start on us, that's for sure. But don't worry, Sam, there's really no place for her to go. We're bound to find her."

Ara ventured a darting glance over the projection of rock. Marc was poised beside an old truck, his back to her. She could see the great width of his shoulders, the ruffled hair, gleaming gold in the sunlight.

Sam Neely paced in front of Marc, then stopped and looked around. His large, bearlike form projected a steely dignity. He stared away from Marc toward the mountains. "She could be anywhere."

"Let me take a look along the beach," Marc said. "You can see for miles down there. That's where I would head if I were her."

Ara's heart sank. If Marc walked down to the shoreline and looked up, he would be bound to spot her. She wouldn't be able to slip over the rise of ridge, for Sam Neely was not likely to leave the vicinity of the truck.

Ara edged herself over toward the brush that clung to the craggy slope. It seemed bare and incapable of concealing her, but it was better than having no shield at all. She flattened herself close against the rocks and waited.

Below her she watched Marc's agile descent. He

stopped beside the lapping water and looked up and down the beach. She held her breath as he turned back.

To her relief his gaze only brushed across the ridge and did not stop on her. She remained without moving, her limbs tense and aching, until Marc was out of sight.

She could hear him saying as he reached the summit, "Let's stop at Barny's place and talk to him. We can get him to run his boat out along the shoreline while we search the interior."

"Good idea—if he's not already off fishing."

So there were a few people living out here after all. That at least gave Ara some hope. She watched the truck disappear, then dropped down along the beach and began walking in the same direction.

Ara soon saw in the distance a man getting ready to set out in a small boat. This must be Barny. She had beaten them to him. Now if only she could convince him to help her.

Her frantic wave caused him to stop all motion.

As she approached, she saw that he was a mature man. Deep creases lined his eyes. His face glowed in the sunlight.

"I must get to Kotzebue," she told him.

He tilted his head and looked puzzled.

He would surely understand Kotzebue. She pronounced it again, very slowly. "I will pay you. I'll give you one hundred dollars if you will take me there."

He grinned. Ara knew he had understood. He lost no time gesturing for her to climb aboard.

''I need to . . . hurry.''

Despite her urgings, he took his time, slowly rearranging his scattered gear. Seated in the narrow boat laden with supplies made Ara feel a little queasy.

Marc and her father would have reached his cabin by now. Soon they would walk down to the shore, looking for him.

''We must hurry!'' Ara repeated anxiously.

Still taking his sweet time, the old man slowly cranked the engine. The motor sputtered and died. Ara wondered how far it was to Kotzebue and if the old craft was up to the trip.

Barny tried the motor again. Why was it taking so long? This time it chugged, but kept running as if missing and ready to rumble at any time to a permanent stop.

Ara glanced anxiously over her shoulder. As she did, she caught sight of Marc and her father hurrying toward them from the direction of the old man's cabin.

Sam's frantic words, carried on the wind, rang out loudly; ''Barny, wait!''

The old man's hand reached out to kill the engine.

''No,'' Ara pleaded. ''Don't listen to them! I have to get back to Kotzebue. Please believe me. My life depends on you!''

The old man's head again tilted, as if he had all the time in the world to weigh and consider her words.

Marc and Ara's father were rapidly closing the space between them. They would reach the boat in a matter of moments.

Just before they did, the ancient fisherman, as if he

hadn't seen or heard them, rammed the craft backward. Clearing the shallow waters near the shore, he spun the boat around with surprising skill and speed. It jolted hard against the waves as it set out toward Kotzebue.

Chapter Fifteen

Ara, lugging her duffel, arrived at the *Sea Rogue* just as the old freighter was making last-minute preparations to launch. As she hurried up the wooden plank, Hal Bruins, distracted from his idle watch, moved forward to block her way. "Do you have a pass?"

"I don't, but I have the captain's permission."

"That won't do. You'll need a pass."

"Let me speak to Captain Riggs."

Hal's pale eyes seemed to mock her. So did the slack lips that slowly stretched into a smile. "He's up in the wheelhouse. Speak to him all you like, but he's not going to let you board."

With growing anxiety Ara hurried up to the top deck. She found Farley Riggs inside the glass enclosure, looking elegant and important as he sorted through a stack of papers.

When he glanced up, Ara thought of how she must look to him. She had rushed to her hotel and picked up her luggage, but she hadn't taken the time to change clothes. She became painfully aware of her oversize sweatshirt and baggy jeans, of the worn boots that no doubt belonged to Sam Neely.

The captain, far too much the gentleman to show that he noticed, asked politely, ''What brings you here, Ara?''

''You said if I ever needed a friend I should see you. I need one now, in the worst way. I must get out of Kotzebue. May I have your permission to go back down the coast on the *Sea Rogue*?''

He hesitated. ''Air flights generally leave Kotzebue every day.''

''I can't wait for that. It's urgent that I leave right now.''

He regarded her, dark eyebrows raised in question. She thought about telling him everything that had happened to her, but she quickly brushed the idea aside. Captain Riggs would demand proof, which she didn't have. But if only he would allow her to board, she would soon have the evidence she so badly needed to back up her story.

The captain still held the papers he had been looking over, but in an absent way, his full attention now focused on Ara's request. She knew that nothing she could say or do was likely to influence him. So she waited, attempting, despite her untidy appearance, to meet his overpowering dignity with a dignity of her own.

Why didn't he answer? Despite her knowledge that Farley Riggs was not a man given to snap decisions, Ara found the long, silent void maddening.

He spoke at last. "You can have your old cabin back."

She breathed a sigh of relief. "Thank you." She started away, then turned back. "I might need a pass to show Hal Bruins."

"Oh, yes, Hal. He's very much the overseer." The captain smiled. "You just go on. I'll get word to him."

Ara felt extremely grateful to the captain as she unpacked her luggage. She took out the camera she had dashed into the general store to purchase. She had bought a Polaroid, so she would have photos as immediate proof of what was taking place on the boat. The first chance she got, before they arrived in Lone Port, she would photograph the contents of the crates. Then, with any luck, she would take shots of Hal Bruins and the men who would arrive at the dock to accept the illegal cargo.

This time Ara would not take the chance of someone stealing her camera. She looked around carefully for a place to hide it. Ara placed the camera in a water pitcher, which she concealed in the storage area that held towels and blankets.

Stepping out of the grungy clothes, Ara opened the shower door and turned on the water. The steady, soothing spray felt heavenly and seemed to wash away the long, terrifying hours. Ara donned a blue blouse and gray slacks and gazed at her image in the mirror. To her dismay she realized that she was still wearing the necklace Marc had purchased for her in Nome. Since he had given it to her, had himself clasped the lock, Ara had not once taken it off.

Ara did so now, quickly, as if the very touch of the necklace against her skin burned her. Ara held it for a moment in her hand before letting it drop to the stand beside the sink. She would miss wearing it. She would miss Marc.

But like the nugget, which wasn't gold at all, nothing about Marc's show of affection for her had been genuine.

Out on deck Ara encountered Curt. He stood leaning against the railing, staring out to sea, his long dark hair blowing in the wind. He looked pensive and solitary.

His hazel eyes lit at the sight of her, as if her appearance was an unexpected but pleasant surprise. "Ara. What are you doing on board?"

"I could ask the same of you," she said, moving forward to join him. "I thought you'd be on your honeymoon."

A look of sadness crossed his face. "The wedding's off. I'm headed back down to Seward, still trying to salvage the business. With all Wayfarer's difficulties, I have plenty to keep me busy, which might be a good thing. At least this emergency trip will help me take my mind off my troubles.''

''What happened between you and Pat?''

''We've split up for good. But maybe it's for the best. I can't just keep fooling myself.''

Ara thought of Marc, and she, too, fell silent, both of them locked in their own private thoughts. Then Curt said, ''We're having a special little dinner party tonight in honor of the captain's birthday. I'm sure he'd be delighted if you would join us.''

''I will be happy to,'' Ara said with an enthusiasm she didn't feel. Curt had suffered a bitter disappointment, and he needed to be with others, to laugh, to relax and enjoy companionship. Ara knew that she needed that, too, even though socializing was the very last thing she felt like doing.

''Good. I'll meet you in the dining room about six-thirty.''

Long after Curt left, Ara remained watching the *Sea Rogue* cut through the gray water. She thought of her father, how she had flown to Alaska with such high hopes. The happy reunion she had expected had turned into one of deceit and terror.

And Marc—Ara's hand automatically rose to the empty place where the large stone had once hung. She wished she had never met him, had never fallen in love with him—Marc, as false as the gold nugget she could no longer bring herself to wear. Tears stung her eyes. Like Curt, Ara knew what it was like to feel hurt, deceived, betrayed.

"You didn't really need to dress up," Curtis said, a twinkle appearing in his hazel eyes. "But I'm glad you did."

With so little choice of clothing, Ara had tried hard to give the illusion of formal wear, selecting a long black skirt and an ivory blouse trimmed with lace. Her efforts, she judged from Curt's admiring look, were well rewarded. He gallantly offered his arm as they passed into the dining area.

Four men sat at the long wooden table. Instead of the tin dishes used ordinarily, fine china gleamed from the white tablecloth. Flickering candles cast long shadows upon the drab gray walls. The touches of glamour amid such shabbiness, as if the dinner were taking place on some fancy cruise liner instead of the *Sea Rogue*, made the scene appear unreal, deceptive.

The captain sat at the head of the table. With his trim gray hair and mustache he cut a striking figure in a dark, well-cut dinner jacket. As he carefully set down his glass, a heavy gold signet ring caught the light and sparkled.

"The last of my special guests have arrived," he said, getting to his feet. "So glad you could join us, Ara."

The three men around him remained in their chairs, Hal Bruins leaning back with a stare grim and hostile.

"Ara, you know Hal, but you probably haven't met my two other right-hand men. This is Danny Grieggs and Buddy Walker."

As he spoke, he gestured to each of them in turn, as if they were wealthy clients or visiting dignitaries.

Ara surveyed the three, thinking they looked like two thugs and a not-too-bright yes-man.

''Welcome,'' the man closest to her, the one the captain had introduced as Danny Grieggs, said, eyeing Ara with a leering boldness. He was bald except for side strands of greasy brown hair.

The other man, Buddy Walker, looked up dully, then lowered his eyes again to the table. A stab of recognition shot through Ara. The big, clumsy-looking man was the sailor Marc had tried to convince her she had mistaken for her father the day she had seen someone disappear into the cargo hold. Up close, with the exception of the broad, bearish shoulders, there was little resemblance between the part-Eskimo giant and Sam Neely.

At the captain's request Ara and Curt seated themselves. Ara glanced around again. She didn't know who she had expected to attend a dinner party on the *Sea Rogue* but rough-hewn sailors. Still, there was something about this trio besides their tacky appearance that made Ara wary.

''A toast to the captain,'' Curtis said, lifting his glass graciously into the air. ''May this birthday gleam long into your memory.''

''Hear, hear,'' the balding man beside him said.

Buddy Walker shifted awkwardly in his chair and remained staring at the table.

''Just how old are you, Cap?'' Hal demanded in his bold, brusque way.

''Compared to the *Sea Rogue*,'' the captain said,

evading the question by flashing a charming smile, "I am just a youngster."

Farley Riggs was so urbane, the epitome of sophistication. Clearly he was accustomed to living the good life. He played the host with a delicate balance, maintaining closeness yet at the same time keeping a distance from his underlings, whose goodwill he would consider necessary to preserving his position and lifestyle.

For a moment Ara felt an alarming wariness of him. She even went so far as to imagine Captain Riggs with a silver loop through his ear, a shining cutlass at his side. It was just as easy to visualize Hal Bruins with a black patch over one eye. The image of Farley Riggs as a modern-day pirate surrounded by his motley crew should have made Ara laugh. Somehow it didn't.

"How many men work on the *Sea Rogue*?" Ara asked.

"Sam sent me out with only a skeleton crew," Farley Riggs answered. "But it takes a big crew to run a ship—"

Hal interrupted, boasting, "Or Hal Bruins."

The captain, smiling over Hal's comment, but not glancing toward him, continued, "These men are my officers. We have a twelve engine hands and deckhands, not to mention the cooks and cleaning staff." He hesitated. "May I have some more wine, please?"

A server, who Ara hadn't seen on board before, sprang forward to fill his glass.

As Farley Riggs slowly sipped the drink, his ring again sent off a glimmer of light. He was obviously a man who appreciated expensive jewelry. Ara thought of her struggle with her attacker in Kotzebue, could again feel the choking pressure of metal against her throat. Her gaze dropped to the captain's wrist, half expecting to see upon it an expensive silver watchband. But the band, like the ring, was gold.

"Will we have a long holdover at Lone Port?" Curt asked.

"Just for one night, same as our last stop there."

Food began arriving. Ara was surprised by the difference between this feast and the ship's daily fare. Salad was followed by baked salmon, rice pilaf, and green beans with slivers of almonds. Ara, Curt, and the captain kept up polite conversation. The other three men ate silently, greedily, their eyes seldom leaving their plates.

"While we're in Lone Port," the captain was saying, "you should make sure Ara meets Noatak." He addressed Ara. "Noatak is the resident artist. His marvelous ivory carvings are worth a small fortune."

Curt looked toward Ara expectantly, but thoughts of Marc, of the wonderful evening they had spent in Lone Port, stifled her response. She did not feel like accepting Curt's unspoken offer or explaining that Noatak and she had already met.

"There are still many ivory carvers," the captain was saying, "but most of them are hacks—illegal ones, at that, not even of Eskimo descent. I would say meeting Noatak is essential. He is the last of a dying breed."

Curt had taken Ara's silence as acceptance. "We'll

go visit Maureen's as soon as we get to Lone Port,''
Curt said. ''Noatak is usually there.''

As they finished the final course, a rich dessert of
Black Forest cake in honor of the captain's birthday,
Ara glanced up to see Hal Bruins's sullen eyes fastened on her. They held a strong message, a warning—
the captain and his three officers were not her friends.
Finding herself suddenly glad for Curt's presence, Ara
moved a fraction of an inch closer to him.

Ara's gaze shifted once more to Captain Riggs, and
she suddenly felt as young Jim Hawkins in *Treasure
Island* must have felt upon discovering Long John Silver's true mission. The realization struck her that upon
escaping Marc and Sam Neely and boarding the *Sea
Rogue*, Ara might have jumped straight from the fry-
ing pan and into the fire.

Ara's suspicions concerning Farley Riggs began to
clear away once Curt and she had left the dining room.
Her fears and speculations had grown all out of pro-
portion because of the way candlelight had flickered
into the semidarkness, by the attempts at eloquence in
so paltry a setting. When she saw Captain Riggs in
daylight again, going about his duties, he would no
longer seem a villain and a fake, and she would no
longer view the evening as a sham.

After all, Curtis, who was, in Sam Neely's absence,
in charge of much of the company's business, seemed
to have no misgivings at all about Captain Riggs or
the officers of the *Sea Rogue.*

Ara wondered as they walked along the deck just

how much she should confide in Curt. If Ara told him what she knew, questions would follow, questions she could not answer. Curtis would have trouble believing that Sam Neely was still alive, that he had attempted to kill her, that he, along with Marc, had kidnapped her. The only way she would be able to convince Curt or anyone else of the criminal activities that were taking place was to supply positive proof. And that, she thought with a sinking heart, was going to be a very dangerous mission.

All of a sudden Curt stopped walking. He gazed down at her, wind blowing through his dark hair. From his sober expression, she gleaned that matters of a different sort weighed heavily on his mind, matters of the heart. Ara knew he must be thinking about the canceled wedding.

Because she had considered him Pat's fiancé, and because of her own infatuation with Marc, Ara had never really noticed except in passing what an attractive man Curtis was. She saw him now as a stranger might see him, sharp, handsome, as her mother would have phrased it, "a boy with potential."

Curtis, as if reluctant to part with Ara, lingered. "If we were in New York, I would have taken you to the opera or to the theater. Imagine, instead, having a first date aboard this old freighter." He paused, then added in a joking manner, "Maybe it'll be a story we'll someday tell our grandkids."

"Grandkids?" She was flirting with him, but at the moment it didn't seem wrong. "You do move fast, don't you?"

Curt's tone became serious. "You fell for him, didn't you? Don't deny it. You were taken in by Marc just like Pat was."

Ara didn't reply.

"You don't have to answer. I know. And it's too soon for either of us to think of romance. But maybe we can be of some solace to each other."

"Like all the old love songs, you mean—work on mending our broken hearts?"

"So that's occurred to you, too?" Curt smiled. "Let's do start seeing one another, Ara. As friends, of course," he added quickly, as if anxious that she should not get the wrong impression.

Ara thought of Marc and knew that right now she did not want to see anyone.

"It's very hard for me," Curt told her earnestly. "You see, I did all I could to make myself into someone Pat could love. I tried to change myself, and that was my mistake. I'm me—not Marc Stewart. I have a feeling it was the real me Pat didn't like, and that's what I couldn't change."

Such a sad, lost look came into Curt's eyes that Ara felt compelled to reach out and touch his arm. "Don't be so hard on yourself, Curt. Maybe Pat just wasn't the right person for you."

Curtis's earnest hazel eyes sought hers. "Did you ever stop to wonder what might have happened if we had met each other instead of them?"

Ara knew Curt did not know her well enough to be speaking these words to her. Hurt by Pat's rejection, he was only acting on the rebound. How easy it would be for her to do the same, to use him to try to forget about Marc.

Curt's lips brushed against hers, surprising her. She felt the gentle pressure of his mouth, barely a kiss at all. His eyes, as they met hers, were full of hope. "Who knows? Maybe we could happen yet."

Chapter Sixteen

With no holdover in Nome, the *Sea Rogue* was making good time sailing back down the coast. Last night at the dinner party the captain had indicated that by late afternoon they would arrive at Lone Port. Ara felt the pressure of his remark and knew she had very little time to find and photograph the old freighter's illegal cargo.

Ara waited until the deck was empty, then kept close to the outside wall until she reached the door marked NO ADMITTANCE. She did not allow herself time to gaze down the shadowy steps, but hurriedly descended into the huge, isolated area enclosed by sea.

Her frightening encounter with Hal Bruins during her last trip into the cargo hold replayed over and over in her mind. She kept expecting at any moment to hear his angry voice, to see him step out in front of her.

The mere thought of that caused her heart to pound. If Hal Bruins found her down here again, armed with her newly purchased Polaroid camera, it would be mean certain death.

Only at the bottom step did Ara feel besieged with doubts concerning the mission itself. The deal she had overheard Willard and Hal Bruins discussing might never have been made. She might find nothing in these wooden storage boxes save ordinary supplies.

Thick canvas bags, wooden crates, packages of all shapes and sizes filled the dank, oily space between her and the wall. Most of them looked innocent enough, contained mail, even odds and ends of furniture.

Ara's gaze skimmed across the stack after stack of wooden crates, all similar to the ones she had seen unloaded at Lone Port. Searching through them all would take hours, hours that she didn't have.

On hands and knees she examined the labels, most of which were clearly marked not only with a number but with a destination. She quickly sorted out the stack of crates stamped LONE PORT.

She rose and looked around. Hanging along the east wall was an assortment tools, some odd and strangely shaped. Beside them were winches and heavy rope that draped down to the floor. Selecting a hammer and a medium-size crowbar, Ara returned to one of the crates and struggled in awkward attempts to pry open the lid.

At last, breathing hard from her effort, Ara felt the wooden top begin to give. She pulled it off and trained her flashlight on what was inside. Pelts. She recognized the snowy white winter coat and black-tipped tail of the Arctic fox. Slate-colored furs, also fox, lay stacked beneath them.

Ara's fingers brushed against a larger pelt, thick and black. Recognition caused her to recoil. She choked back a sense of shock and bitterness as a vision of the proud black wolf she had seen caged at Marc's cabin leaped to mind. Had Marc lied to Pat, as well as to her, about setting the black wolf free? Even though this wasn't that particular wolf, the thought came to her that Marc would have no qualms about slaughtering and skinning the animal she had seen for its magnificent pelt.

Regardless of whether or not the furs had been taken according to government guidelines, the thought that Marc had played any part in this sickened her.

Beneath fox and wolf furs lay an abundance of darkish brown mink pelts. Ara frowned. Although there were strict regulations concerning the trapping of these animals, none of them, as far as she knew, were endangered species. However personally appalling she might find the practice, the transport of these pelts could be perfectly legal.

Ara moved over to the next crate. She had started to open it when the sound of heavy footsteps caused her hand to freeze in midair.

Ara didn't have time to fasten the lid, but she replaced it and ducked back behind a large piece of furniture tied with a packing blanket.

Muffled conversation grew louder and became

clear. She recognized Hal Bruins's voice saying, "I've just checked with the old man. He says we're going to be running late. He doesn't expect us to get to Lone Port until after dark. It's dark for such a short time, we're going to have to work fast."

"That's not our biggest problem. We have to think of the other boat. We don't want them waiting for us with open arms." Ara took this speaker to be Danny Grieggs, who she had met at the captain's party. The thought of his balding head, rimmed by greasy hair, of his leering eyes, a match for Hal's in evilness, made her shrink even farther away from them.

"We'll signal the boat to make sure they stay out until after we dock. Then we've got to be quick about the transport. You be sure everything's ready on this end." Hal Bruins had stepped closer to Ara's hiding place. Only the tall crate separated them. She dared not make a move.

Suddenly Hal burst out, "What's this?"

Ara held her breath. Hal must have discovered the loose lid. He would surely know just who had been tampering with the cargo and would begin at once to search for her.

"I almost tripped over this."

Ara had been wrong. Hal must merely have stumbled into the hammer Ara had in her haste forgotten to hide.

"How many times do I have to tell you? You take a tool; you put it back."

"It weren't me that left that hammer there," Grieggs replied petulantly.

Hal paid no attention to Grieggs's adamant denial. "Carelessness is something I can't put up with. Every little detail must be seen to flawlessly. If it isn't, we could all end up in the slammer." Hal's voice became lower in volume as his reprimand continued. He must have crossed the room to replace the hammer. "I wonder just how many times I have to tell you that?"

"Must have been Buddy that left it there. I think he gets dumber every day."

"He's stupid, all right. And you can't trust stupid. I wasn't happy when he signed on. In fact, I wish he wasn't a part of our little operation. I think this is going to be his last trip."

"Captain likes him."

"Captain might like him ever so well, but Hal Bruins runs the ship. Don't ever forget that. Now where did you put that list I told you not to let out of your sight?"

"Here it is, right where I left it."

To Ara's relief the sound of footsteps diminished. She crouched where she was for a while longer, then slowly edged her way out. For a long time as her nervous hands worked with the crowbar, she couldn't shake the feeling that someone remained in the cargo hold. She kept glancing around, half-convinced that eyes from some dark, hidden recess were fastened steadily upon her.

But that was impossible. She had heard them both leave.

Ara went after the hammer again, for it was smaller and easier to use. She pulled out the final nail that held the lid. Inside were more furs just like the ones in the last box.

But from Hal Bruins's and Danny Grieggs's remarks, Ara knew the illegal goods existed. But how long was it going to take her to find them?

As she pushed aside a few of the snow white furs, Ara's hand brushed against something hard and smooth. What she saw made her draw back with a gasp of surprise. Beneath the thin covering of pelts were row upon row of uncarved walrus tusks.

Ara remembered the captain telling her that the transporting of uncarved ivory was strictly forbidden. She stared down at the tusks, knowing she had located at least some of the contraband.

Ivory from Kotzebue—no telling what the other crates held from other destinations. This discovery was no doubt only the tip of the iceberg. The tramp ship the *Sea Rogue*, with its stops at remote ports up and down the coast, was being used for the illegal export of Alaska's treasures.

Ara quickly snapped pictures, then carefully replaced the lid, securing it tightly before she opened the one beside it.

This crate was packed to the brim with sleek, dark furs that shone silver in the beam from her flashlight. The rich, lustrous fur felt supple to her touch. Seal fur, she thought, likely from baby seals. Whoever had put together this deal had gone for value, for the contents of this crate were certain to bring top money.

The ugly image of greed left Ara seething with anger. Whoever had filled these crates, or had handled them, for that matter, had no respect for life, had no respect for the law that strictly forbade this massive and senseless slaughter of Alaskan wildlife.

Ara had to force herself to focus on taking the necessary photographs, making certain to include in some of the pictures the surrounding area, the metal side hung with tools, for she needed to be able to identify the ship as the *Sea Rogue*. Just as she had finished with the last shot, Ara heard a faint shuffling noise from behind her.

Someone had been watching her. She whirled around, and at the same time, the man did, too. Ara's gaze fell across a broad back with wide, massive shoulders.

Sam Neely.

Chapter Seventeen

Attempting to reach the door, but knowing he had been spotted, he drew to a lumbering stop. Slowly, like some clumsy animal poising for attack, surprised and confused by her presence, he faced her.

Ara had once again mistaken the bearish Buddy Walker for her father.

His blunt features showed no anger or threat. Only fear registered in the dull eyes that met hers briefly, then shifted quickly away.

"Buddy."

At the calling of his name, he shuffled back closer to the door. He seemed to have only one concern: getting away from her.

Hal and Danny Grieggs had referred to him as stupid. If he wasn't, he was at best painfully slow and backward. Unlike his two companions, he did not look evil: in fact, Ara thought she could appeal to him, the same way she would appeal to a small child. "Buddy, I wish you wouldn't tell Hal that you saw me here."

His words had a timorous break as he said, "You shouldn't be opening those boxes. They don't belong to you."

"I'm not doing anything wrong. But they are, Buddy. And you are too, if you help them."

He shuffled uneasily.

"They're not your friends, Buddy. Don't let them tell you what to do anymore. Not even tonight, with the unloading of these crates. Don't go along with it. Tell them you're sick."

Ara couldn't believe that in this circumstance she would find herself trying to save him, but he looked so vulnerable she could not help herself. "They're just using you, Buddy. They don't care at all if you get into serious trouble."

His blank stare left her feeling uncertain. Did he even understand what she was trying to tell him?

Without another word, Buddy darted toward the door.

"Buddy."

He didn't stop, not even to glance around. No doubt he was going directly to Hal Bruins.

If he did, Ara would never reach Lone Port alive.

Ara had intended to photograph the men in the process of accepting the illegal shipment. Now that was far too risky. She had to come up with another plan. But what could it be, and was there enough time left?

The answer came to her clearly. She had no choice but to trust someone. If she were the only one who knew what her father and his select helpers were doing, if some ill fate should befall her, then the smugglers would succeed and would be able to keep on with their illegal operations.

Ara knew she had to take a chance. The logical person to confide in, to take the photographs to, would be Captain Riggs.

Ara cautiously stepped out on deck and lingered there for a moment in grave consideration. The last lowering rays of sunlight sent out penetrating beams across the smooth sea. But along the shoreline the sheltering coves and jutting rocks were cast with shadows. The few hours of Alaskan darkness would fall very soon, before she was prepared for it.

Ara passed no one as she climbed the stairs to the upper deck. Still hesitant, she stopped in the doorway of the wheelhouse, where Farley Riggs stood alone near the controls.

He seemed deeply absorbed in some task, and she did not want to interrupt him. Even in solitude, even though his back was to her, he possessed the same elegant, in-charge bearing.

It took her some time to realize what he was doing.

Ara remained rooted in the doorway, as if frozen in place, and watched blinking gleams of light break against the still, dusky sky. Two short bursts followed by a long one.

Farley Riggs, with an air of magnificent patience, persisted with the signaling. At last Ara spied a flash-

ing beam that responded in exactly the same way—
two short flashes, one long one.

The captain, satisfied that he had made contact with
the other ship, immediately discontinued his work. He
stepped back from the control boards, halting in surprise when he saw Ara.

Hal Bruins had said the ship that would receive the
contraband would be signaled before they arrived at
port. That was exactly what the captain was doing. She
had made a dreadful mistake getting back on this boat.
Now she had nowhere to run and no one to turn to.

Farley Riggs gazed at her quietly, a clever man. No
doubt he had already guessed why she had come to
him. Still he said in an affable way, "Is there something I can do for you, Ara?"

She had to think fast. "I wanted to tell you that I
intend to stay in Lone Port for a few days."

Her announcement, as usual, merited his full attention. "Maureen would rent you a room," he said help-
fully. Then he smiled. "But a few hours of Lone Port
is quite enough for most people."

"I just wanted to let you know," Ara said, and
backed away from him, far out into the upper deck.

Then she whirled and fled down the steps.

Ara's knees felt weak, and she was breathing very
hard by the time she reached the lower level. She was
certain now that they all knew she had uncovered their
lawless scheme. Soon they would be closing in on her.
She had no one but herself to blame. She had placed
herself in the very heart of danger.

Ara set out in the same rapid pace toward the back

deck, then stopped short. Already men were bringing up the illegal cargo. Hal Bruins, not lifting a hand in assistance, stood squarely between Danny Grieggs and a man she didn't know. Ara had stepped out into full view of them. Terrified that Hal Bruins had seen her, Ara shrank back against the metal wall.

At that very moment, like the last minute twist of a steering wheel to avert a wreck, she thought of Curt. Curt Carter was her last and only chance.

She threw open the door to the dining room and met him face-to-face. Dressed in a white shirt and pleated trousers, Curt looked every bit the aspiring young executive, strong and responsible. The unexpected sight of him almost caused her to sob in relief.

He laid down the papers he was holding and pushed his dark-tinted reading glasses up across his forehead. The action swept dark hair away from his face, accentuating his lean features.

Ara started to say, ''I'm so glad to see you!'' but Curt's raised arm had tugged the shirtsleeve away from his wrist, leaving revealed the thick silver watchband he wore.

The sight of it stopped her words. In the electric silence, Ara felt once again the choking pain of cold, heavy metal against her throat. She stared at him in disbelief.

Her father had not been the one who had pushed her from the *Arctic Belle*. Marc and Sam Neely had been watching the Wayfarer office for the same reason she had; to find out who was dealing with the Eskimo for his black-market goods.

Her father and Marc had saved her life, had taken her to the cabin, had wanted to keep her safely there. The only two people who would help her, she had left far behind—to reboard a ship of dangerous criminals.

Ara attempted to avert her eyes from his, but it was way too late. He had already read the horror and accusation she was helpless to hide.

Curt's whole appearance changed. Coldness crept into his hazel eyes. His thin lips tightened into a cruel line.

He had shed the role of the sensitive, rejected lover as easily as a snake shed its skin. The hardness of his features made him seem like another person, one she was meeting for the first time. In that moment Ara caught a glimpse of what Pat must have seen, what must have made her have doubts all along about marrying him. She saw the insincerity, the hypocrisy, the *evil* behind the chameleonlike facade.

But not in time—she now had no possible means of escape. Curt and everyone else on board the *Sea Rogue* was part of the operation.

"Sam gave you a trusted position. How could you do this to him?"

Ara had been referring to his reaping financial rewards on the side, but that was not what Curt addressed.

"I had to kill him," he said. "That was his fault, not mine. I was perfectly content with the money I was making. Then Sam figured out that the *Sea Rogue* was being used for smuggling. I couldn't let him find out I was the head of it, now, could I?"

"You mean he never actually found out about you?"

"He would have. It was only a matter of time. Sam kept on snooping around and finally found our warehouse in Nome. While he was opening one of our crates, I slipped in, struck him over the head, and killed him. Then I got the idea that if I placed his body in his boat and set him adrift, his death would be considered an accident."

As Curt spoke, he stepped closer, closing the space between them.

"Come with me," he said in a low, controlled voice. "We're going down into the cargo hold." He reached around her and opened the door, forcing her ahead of him out onto the deck.

He had made two attempts to kill her. This time he would succeed. But not without a struggle. Ara, amazed at her own calm sense of control, shook her hand free of his and backed away from him.

Curt took a small gun from his pocket and leveled it at her. "We are going down to the cargo hold," he repeated.

If she were to die anyway, it might just as well be now—with a shot in the back. At least he would never be able to make that look like an accident.

For a second she stood immobile, aware of the old freighter cutting through the water, aware of the cry of gulls overhead. She drew in her breath, knowing this was going to be the end. Then she whirled and began running.

To her surprise no bullets zinged after her. Panic

increased her speed. She could hear the rapid fall of Curt's footsteps behind her.

The captain was a robber, but maybe he wasn't a murderer. She put a last effort into her flight, almost reaching the steps to the upper deck before Curt caught her.

They locked in fierce struggle. Little by little he gained advantage. She could not break the iron grip of his hands. With sheer brute force Curt dragged her backward along the deck toward the door to the cargo hold.

He stopped her near the railing, twisting her head down so she faced the churning sea. "That will be your grave," he said, "but not yet. Not until we are unloaded and set out again."

He pivoted her around toward the door marked NO ADMITTANCE, shoving her roughly down the steps into the dank storage area—the place where he intended to kill her.

The dim light added a viciousness to his features. The barrel of the gun was pointed at her heart.

"How could you do this to Pat?" Ara asked with contempt. "The only reason you wanted to marry her was because she was Sam Neely's legal heir. All you ever wanted was to get control of Wayfarer Charters."

Curt's look darkened. "And then I found out about you. I read one of your letters to Sam where you mentioned meeting him on this ship. When you showed up asking about Sam I knew you were his long-lost daughter." He added with a rueful laugh, "Your showing up really threw a monkey wrench in my plans. My fiancé would no longer be in line to inherit Wayfarer Charters. You would.''

Ara had known from the first that the attempt made on her life had not sprung from the smugglers. She had been no real threat to them at the time. She had thought of her father, but had never once considered Curt's motive. The way Curt was pressuring Pat to marry him should have given her some clue.

''So you tried to arrange an 'accident' before anyone else made the connection that I was Sam's daughter.''

''You're exactly right.''

''But things didn't go quite the way you planned.''

A bitter, ironic smile crossed Curt's lips. ''I'd say everything that could possibly go wrong did. You didn't die in the 'accident' I arranged for you aboard the *Sea Rogue*, Sam's body didn't wash ashore with the boat, and worst of all, Pat jilted me at the altar.''

Ara had been right in his office when he had talked to Hal Bruins about the deal with Willard. ''You were the one hiding on the *Arctic Belle* that night.''

''When I spotted Marc, I knew it was a setup. I knew Marc had somehow found out about the meeting. I headed for cover. I didn't know anyone else was aboard the old ship, not until I ran into you. At that time I still believed that Pat was going to marry me, and so there I was, presented with the perfect opportunity.''

''So you pushed me overboard.''

''I must admit I was surprised when you turned up again on the *Sea Rogue*.''

"But at that point, you decided not to kill me."

"A simple change in strategy. Since you were Sam's true heir, I figured I could get control of the company just as easily by marrying you."

"You thought you'd turn what you did to Sam to your advantage. You'd marry his heir and get full control of his company . . . one that never was in any financial trouble."

"All it would have taken was a little patience. And the wait wouldn't have been that unpleasant. We might even have been happy together if you hadn't found out about the smuggling."

"I would never have married you."

Curtis replied, unmoved, "It doesn't matter now. Since you know everything I've done, I can't let you live." The gun wavered a little in his hand. "Whether Sam's body is ever found or not, with you eliminated, Pat is still in charge of the company. She'll come around. All I have to do is bring her a bouquet of flowers, patch up our differences." His hand tightened on the gun. "My luck's bound to turn. What else could possibly go wrong?"

"Only one thing I can think of," Ara replied. "Sam Neely isn't dead."

Curtis's eyes widened. "That's impossible!"

"Is it?" From the edges of surrounding darkness, a huge, burly form emerged.

Sam Neely strode boldly forward until he stood between Curt and Ara, a human shield, his powerful, bearlike form protecting Ara from harm.

Curt's face turned ashen, as if he had seen a ghost.

Then a slow smile played across his lips. The point of the gun now aimed, not at Ara, but at her father.

''I killed you once,'' Curt said threateningly. ''I can kill you again.''

Chapter Eighteen

Out of the corner of her eye, Ara saw what Curtis didn't—a figure moving forward with silent, catlike speed. Marc!

With great difficulty Ara forced her attention to remain on Curt, whose gaze had momentarily shifted from her father to her. "Now you can both die together."

Sam Neely had known all along Marc would be entering through the opposite door. "You've committed a crime," he said, his booming voice a distraction, "but so far it isn't murder."

The word *murder* had barely escaped his lips when Marc struck. Ara saw the image of his strong hands locked on Curt's wrist, saw the barrel of the gun wrench upward.

Her father stopped her from bounding forward. As

the two men struggled, he, against Ara's will, pulled her away from the danger of the wavering gun barrel.

A sharp clack sounded as metal hit against the floor. Sam sprang forward to retrieve the gun, but too late. Curt, closer to it, reached it first. He grabbed it and scrambled to his feet.

Ara held her breath.

The barrel of gun waved back and forth from Sam to Marc. The instant it returned to Sam, Marc dived forward. The two crashed back against a stack of crates. The gun went off with a jarring blast.

Marc, gaining possession of the weapon, hurled it away from them, back into the sea of cargo. At that same moment a clatter of footsteps sounded on the stairway.

Captain Riggs, followed by several men wearing the uniform of the Coast Guard, burst into the cargo hold.

Captain Riggs's stern voice rang into the silence, as explosive as the bullet had been. "It's all over, Carter. We've already got Hal Bruins and the rest of your gang in custody."

Instead of looking defeated, Curt stared defiantly at Farley Riggs and the armed men behind him. Then his gaze settled on Ara, and he spoke with great contempt. "I always kept safely out of the way. They never would have found out that I was the head man, if it weren't for you."

Ara, planning to meet her father at Maureen's for breakfast—hoping Marc would be there, too—stopped at the gangplank to talk to the captain.

"I thought I saw Buddy Walker this morning. Didn't they take him into custody, too?"

The captain's thin eyebrows rose in question. "Strange thing, Buddy wasn't with the men who loaded the cargo last night. Consequently, there was no reason to arrest him." Farley Riggs paused. "Buddy took orders from Hal. Poor Buddy takes orders from everyone. He's not really guilty of much else."

Ara started away, then turned back. "When I came up to talk to you, I thought you were signaling to the smugglers."

"On the contrary," the captain said with a smile. "I was signaling to Sam and Marc. After Sam was attacked and believed dead, he contacted me. He asked me to take over as captain of the *Sea Rogue* and work with him and Marc. We knew goods were being smuggled. We knew Hal Bruins was involved, which is how we found out about the meeting at Wayfarer Charters. We could have gotten them at any time, but we wanted to stop this once and for all, to get the ringleader."

"I'm glad," Ara said, "that you turned out to be on our side. I only wish I had known it sooner."

"I was tempted to tell you, but then I had to keep my promise to Sam. He insisted that the more we told you, the more danger you would be in."

Ara hurried off anxious to meet her father.

Maureen called to Ara as she entered the café, "The handsome lug is right over there. Hope you're hungry. He's ordered a breakfast for you that you wouldn't believe."

Ara slipped into the bench across from him. Sam Neely took a drink of coffee, gazing at her over the rim of the cup. "All these years, I never knew I had a daughter," he told her. "Rhonda and I kept in contact. Our plan was to remarry the moment she was of age. I guess she didn't tell me about you because she knew there wouldn't have been any waiting if I knew." A sad look flickered across his face. "Then I heard she was killed in that accident." He didn't speak for a long time. "You look like your mother, you know. Even though you act more like me."

Ara laughed. "When you didn't show up on the *Sea Rogue*, I thought you had changed your mind about wanting to meet me. I almost turned around and went back to Montana."

"Since I couldn't meet you myself, I contacted Marc to make sure you stayed safe. He was supposed to convince you to go back home. But you refused to listen. I never counted on you inheriting my stubbornness."

His kindly gaze held hers as he continued, "Believe me, I never meant to involve you in all this. After I sent you the pass, I found the warehouse in Nome. Curt knew I would trace the renting of the building back to him, so he decided he would be better off with me out of the way. You know, I never even suspected him. When I contacted Pat, I told her to do whatever she wanted to about the marriage. It was Marc who tried to stop it."

"You must have been hurt very badly for Curt to have thought you were dead."

"For a long time, the boat drifted. I was found by an Eskimo fisherman, a friend of mine, and he took me in. For days I was delirious. By the time I had recovered enough to realize what had happened, I tried to contact you. But you had already left Montana."

"I came to Alaska early," Ara said. "I had a job interview at Lake Clark National Park. I was offered the position of biological technician, but I told them I needed some time to think it over."

"Good. Because I have a better job offer." His speculative eyes held hers. "For a long time now, I've been thinking of starting a wildlife refuge center near Nome. Of course, that's Pat and Marc's idea as well as mine. We could really use someone with your education to help get the center off the ground." He added with growing enthusiam, "How about it, Ara? Would you consider coming to work for me instead?"

Ara felt a surge of joy. To have the perfect job in her field, to be around her father; it was almost too good to be true. Only one thing was wrong—she might not be able to bear working side-by-side with Marc and Pat. Now that Curt was out of the picture, they were bound to become a couple again. And the way she felt about Marc . . .

Ara tried to keep the sadness from her voice as she asked, "Where is Marc? I thought he'd join us for breakfast."

Unaware of Ara's feelings for Marc, Sam said, "He went after Pat. When we contacted her last night, she said she'd catch a charter flight into Lone Port. They should be here any minute."

Ara steeled herself for the sight of Marc and Pat together, laughing, holding hands.

Before she could prepare herself, she heard the sound of their voices.

Pat rushed forward to hug Sam, then Ara, saying to her, ''I want us to be just like sisters.'' She addressed Marc. ''You've always been like a brother to me. You don't mind, do you, if I add a sister?''

''You couldn't choose a better one,'' Marc said.

''Go on,'' Pat encouraged. ''Ask her. All she can do is say no.''

''Better try,'' Marc replied, a little shyly. ''What else can I do?'' He turned to Ara, saying, ''When you ran away from that cabin, I realized how I felt about you. I never want to lose you again!'' As he spoke, Marc reached into his pocket and drew out a small, velvet-covered box.

As Ara opened the lid, she gave a little cry of surprise and delight. A lovely engagement ring caught the light and glittered.

''A little present for you,'' Marc said. ''I hope you'll accept it. And me, too,'' he added with a smile. ''I go along with it.''

Marc slipped the ring on her left finger, where it fit perfectly. Ara glanced from her father to Pat, both beaming and happy. Then her eyes met Marc's deep blue ones.

''It's not like the other gift I gave you,'' he said. ''This time the gold is genuine.''